# Melting the Snow

Authors:
Lindsey Gray
Michele Richard

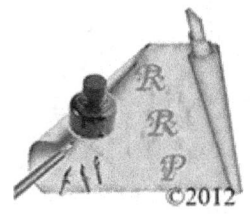

Melting the Snow

# Melting the Snow

Published by
Renaissance Romance Publishing

ISBN-13:
978-0615940991 (Renaissance Romance Publishing)

ISBN-10:
0615940994

Cover Art info:
Cover Design by: Melissa Conder

# Melting the Snow

# Stories:

# Holiday Cure for the Cursed
# &
# Frozen Moments

# Melting the Snow

# Holiday Cure for the Cursed

By

Lindsey Gray

# Melting the Snow

## *Dedication:*

Thank you to my older sister, Renea, for letting me tag along on her school trip to New York City. That trip gave me my first look at the Big Apple, an experience I will never forget.

# Melting the Snow

# Contents

# Melting the Snow

# Prologue

"Men suck." CiCi Newport blew a lock of her brunette hair away from her face before gulping the rest of her champagne.

"Not all men, I hope."

She glanced over in the direction from which the male voice had come. It was taking her a few seconds to focus in her inebriated state. After her lids blinked a few times over her pale green eyes, she was able to see the person before her.

Large feet were encased in knee high, black, leather boots with shiny silver buckles. Red velvet trousers were neatly tucked into the top of each boot. A matching red velvet coat with intricate silver buttons and white fur trim fit snug around his round belly. A real beard of snow-white wisps fell to the middle of his chest. The same white hair flowed from his head and curled above his shoulders. His small smile, which was accompanied by his rosy cheeks and twinkling blue eyes, made her believe she was staring at the genuine article.

"Santa?" she questioned with a slight slur.

"For the purpose of this conversation, let's say that is true." He pulled out a chair and took a seat. All the partygoers from the annual Christmas Gala held in her late father's honor had taken their leave. Only CiCi and Santa were remaining. "What seems to be troubling you, dear?"

She placed her empty champagne flute on the table with a sniffle and launched into the story of her last few days.

"I know I have no right to complain. I have friends and family I love. I have enough money to live more than comfortably for the rest of my life. Tonight was supposed to be the beginning of my happily ever after." A tear ran down her cheek.

Santa pulled a handkerchief from his coat pocket and offered it to her.

"Thanks." She wiped the soft cloth beneath her eyes.

"Looks as though someone gave you something to complain about."

She nodded before she began. "I met Jensen at this gala two years ago. We've been inseparable since. There were hints for months that he was going to propose tonight. Three days ago, I found out he cleaned out my personal safe. He stole my mother's jewelry, emergency cash, and some mementos from my father. It's all gone. I found out this morning he's been arrested. Turns out he's been seeing another woman for over a year, and they've been planning this for months. And to top it off, I had to explain his absence all night and hear how much he was missed. I smiled and nodded like a fool."

"Hence the 'men suck' comment."

"Yeah." CiCi turned her head to find an open champagne bottle on the table. She was tempted to pour herself another glass, but Santa took her hand in his.

"I know things seem bleak now, but you will find love when you least expect it. Christmas can be a magical time of year. Wondrous things can happen."

CiCi let out a soft laugh. "But how will I know he wants me for me and not my money?"

"Your heart will know, dear."

Her heart would know. The heart that lay in pieces in her chest felt beyond repair. How could she trust any man not to damage it any further?

"You'll find him, and when you do, this feeling will be nothing but a memory."

She nodded before he brought her in for a hug, leaving behind the memory of soft velvet on her wet cheek.

The next morning, it all seemed like a dream. Crying on Santa's shoulder couldn't have been real, could it? It did give her an idea, though. She grabbed her sketchbook from her bedside table and began the long road toward her newest creation.

# Melting the Snow

# Chapter One

**One year, ten months, and two weeks later . . .**

"Why do I let you talk me into these things?" Daniel Digby moaned when he was handed another shot of whiskey.

"You need to celebrate. It's the holidays, and you finally have this sexual harassment crap behind you. It's time to move on with your life." Daniel's best friend, Gabe, took another shot and slapped him on the back.

His friend was right. Daniel had battled through the sexual harassment lawsuit he had brought against his former employer. Now that he had settled the case, it was time to take the position he had been offered as a senior consultant at Henderson Public Relations.

"I know. I know." He drank his own shot and winced at the slight burn when he swallowed. "It was the second job I've had to leave because of harassment. This Henderson job is a great opportunity. I've got to make it work."

Daniel couldn't help his appearance. He looked like the green-eyed younger brother of Nathan Fillion. At six foot one, he was even the same height as the well-known actor. With what women deemed 'luscious' brown hair and six-pack abs, he was a magnet for unwanted sexual attention. Sexual overtures from his former superior had been blatant throughout their working relationship. The last straw had come when she entered his office while he was asleep on his couch. She'd locked the door behind her and tried to take full advantage of the situation. Thank God his personal assistant, Samantha, had come into work early that morning and gotten to him in the nick of time.

"I've got it!" Gabe slammed his shot glass on the bar top.

"Oh, God," Daniel groaned. Ideas that popped into Gabe's mind were, more often than not, bad ones.

"Pretend to be married. Get a ring and the whole shebang."

Daniel was caught unawares. Become unavailable. Romantic encounters, if he ever had any, would have to be kept separate from his work life. At this point, he was ready to give about anything a try.

"I guess I'm going ring shopping."

~*~*~

"You know I don't date. I don't have time or any viable options." CiCi Newport spoke to her sister on her cell phone while she walked down her front stoop. She pulled her heavy wool coat tight around her before she set off with her large, leather portfolio in tow.

"I'm worried. You're out there all alone. I want you to find someone."

"Bridgett, if I find someone who wants me for more than my name or the size of my bank account, it'll be a miracle." She continued to walk toward her favorite coffee shop.

Life in her late father's shadow could be bleak at times. His ingenuity and brilliance in the field of technology had netted him billions of dollars over his lifetime. Half of those billions now belonged to her. What he had worked so hard to give her, a life without struggle or want, left her unable to get the one thing money couldn't buy: love.

"I wish you'd move to L.A. Aren't you tired of the cold winters yet?"

Bridgett's distain for New York was obvious. She'd been nineteen when CiCi was born to their father and CiCi's mother. Already hard at work toward a degree at UCLA, Bridgett had missed a majority of CiCi's childhood. It was only after both her parents had passed on, her mother when she was twelve and her father after she turned sixteen, that CiCi connected with her only sibling. CiCi spent her last two years of high school with her sister, brother-in-law, niece, and two nephews in L.A. before she returned to New York City to attend NYU.

"You know how much I love the snow. It's

November, and we've already had plenty of it." The snow crunched beneath her feet while she spoke, yet the air was warmer than normal after a snowfall. "I'm getting my coffee; then I'm off to my publisher's for a meeting. Can I call you later?"

"I might be taking the dogs for a walk on the beach, so text me."

"Ha, ha. Funny." Bridgett knew that particular activity was one of CiCi's favorite pastimes whenever she lived in or visited L. A.

They said their goodbyes before CiCi entered Villanova Coffee. It wasn't her favorite coffee spot because it was only a few blocks from her brownstone. The appeal came from the welcoming atmosphere of red velvet chairs and the best Colombian coffee outside of Colombia.

The warmth and aroma greeted her like an old friend as she walked to the counter to place her order.

Nicki, the barista, gave her a cheerful greeting. "Hey, CiCi. Want me to whip up a peppermint mocha for you?"

"You know me too well." CiCi smiled, pulled out some cash, and passed over the fee she always paid. Even though Thanksgiving hadn't arrived, with her new Christmas book coming out, she was in the mood for her favorite winter drink.

CiCi noticed Nicki freeze when a man

cleared his throat. The barista's brown eyes went wide as saucers. When CiCi noticed what had caught her attention, her own eyes widened.

Tall, with dark brown hair and tailored everything, he looked up to stare at the menu board, and heaven help her, she believed she might faint. A pair of piercing green eyes scanned the board.

Nicki got herself under control and prepared CiCi's order before she returned to take the mystery man's.

"How may I help you?" she asked nervously

"I don't see peppermint mocha on the menu."

"It's not," Nicki said while batting her eyelashes. "I keep a stash of peppermint for some of our regular customers. I can make you one if you'd like."

"Great. Make it a large, please."

CiCi let out a little laugh. It wasn't hard to believe he had charmed Nicki's secret peppermint stash out of her. The man looked at CiCi for a moment before turning to pay and collect his coffee. She propped her portfolio beside the chair and removed her gloves, scarf, and coat. The feel of the rich velvet of the chair through her black, cashmere sweater and her thick, gray trousers was something she had to experience in order to function the rest of the day.

"Did you find something amusing about my order?"

CiCi looked to see the man standing beside her chair.

"No, sorry. I had ordered the same thing. It's what I always order."

"It's good?"

"The best," she replied with confidence.

He took a tentative sip, then a larger one. "It's like liquid Christmas."

"I hope that's a good thing."

"The best. I love Christmastime: the food, the music; everything except the shopping, of course." He took another sip and sighed in contentment. "I might have to make this my morning coffee stop."

"It's been mine for as long as I can remember, if that's any recommendation." A slight blush warmed her cheeks; she was unable to believe she was flirting with the Adonis that shared her coffee preference.

"Maybe I'll see you around?" His eyebrows lifted with his question.

CiCi wondered if by some miracle he was flirting back. It wasn't something she was used to, so she couldn't be sure based on this first meeting. If she wanted there to be a second, she realized, she would have to answer his question.

"If you come around this time, I would say there is a pretty good chance you'll catch me." She smiled and noticed he returned her smile with a smidgen of excitement.

"Tomorrow?"

"Tomorrow," she replied.

He lifted his cup to her with another smile, and then was on his way.

Her heart fluttered in her chest at the thought of tomorrow. Could she? Would she?

Right then, she made a vow to herself. If she saw him again, she would get to know the man before her family name came into play. Maybe, just maybe, she would find a man who wanted *her* more than he wanted her money.

# Melting the Snow

# Chapter Two

"These are amazing," Lori Faison, CiCi's publisher, gushed.

"Thanks. You think everything will be ready on time?" CiCi was always stressed about deadlines since she was now pulling double duty as a children's author *and* illustrator. She had illustrated twelve books, but this one was her second as an author as well. Her first solo project, "Santa's Shoulder," would be released a few weeks before Christmas.

"Will you stop worrying? Relax; it's in the bag." Lori dismissed CiCi's obvious nerves. "Oh, I forgot to tell you about the marketing problem."

"Problem?" CiCi swallowed hard, and her pulse began to race. Lori should have known better than to bring up anything that might push CiCi over the edge.

"Basically, the PR firm we have been using got shut down. Some tax thing or other such nonsense. We've decided to do all our marketing with Henderson PR. You know Phillip Reese, right?"

"Yes, we met at a fundraiser I was chairing for the Literacy Assistance Center a few years ago. We've kept in touch." One of the many perks of being the daughter of the late Winston Newport was being able to support causes she really cared about. Her father never backed anything unless he believed in the cause.

"Good. He's in charge over there now. I've been assured he will personally handle your account."

CiCi nodded, taking it all in. She wasn't worried, since she had every faith in Phillip's abilities.

"So, now you have a few weeks downtime, what are you going to do?" Lori asked with a raised eyebrow.

"Nothing scandalous. My niece, Emily, and her family are coming for Thanksgiving. I'll be working on baby-proofing the brownstone for her two-year-old son. I'm sure it will take me a week, maybe two, to get it done."

"Dear, isn't that what you have Reggie and Marcy for?" Lori rolled her eyes at the thought of CiCi doing housework.

"I like doing these things for myself. Reggie and Marcy have enough on their plates keeping the brownstone together. They don't need extra work added on that I can take care of myself."

Reggie had been the Newport Family butler since CiCi was five. Marcy came along when CiCi's mother became too ill to take care of the housekeeping and cooking. The two had the house to themselves while CiCi was in California. Two years alone had allowed the middle-agers to become better acquainted with each other. They were married CiCi's freshman year in college and now had most of the fourth floor to themselves.

"I wish I had someone to take care of the disaster festering in *my* house." Lori quipped. "Have a good holiday, and we'll talk soon."

CiCi took those words to mean she'd been dismissed, and she wished Lori a good holiday as well.

When CiCi entered the elevator, she began thinking of her mystery man from the coffee shop. Thoughts of tomorrow flooded her mind. The one that kept hitting her over and over was the question of what she would wear.

~*~*~

Daniel toyed with the foreign ring on his left hand while he sat at his new desk. He had gone through with Gabe's plan, but after the chance meeting with the beautiful, green-eyed brunette at the coffee shop that morning, he wasn't sure how it would all work out. Thankfully, he'd remembered to put the ring on before he entered the building. Several women had checked out his left hand when he was introduced to the rest of the staff. He felt relief when he saw disappointment in their eyes.

Daniel had been brought up to speed on the accounts to which he had been assigned by lunchtime. He used his time at the beginning of the afternoon to daydream about his new favorite coffee spot. Not only was the coffee phenomenal, but he imagined the company would be, also. He found himself optimistic about the possibility of tomorrow.

"How was your first day?"

Daniel looked to see his new boss, Phillip Reese, standing in the office doorway.

"Good. I think I made some real headway. I was thinking we should discuss a few things for the holidays."

"Sure," Phillip answered. "Get with my assistant tomorrow, and she'll get you on my schedule."

"I will. Thank you again for this opportunity and for letting me bring Samantha with me." He had felt horrible that when his personal assistant had saved him, she'd put her own job on the line. Phillip didn't seem to have any problem with the package deal. Samantha Wiggins had started several weeks before Daniel to get used to the new company and staff.

"We're glad to have you both, Daniel." Phillip smiled, but then furrowed his brow. "I didn't realize you were married."

"Oh, yes." Daniel fiddled with his ring. "Just recently. Still not used to wearing it."

"Congratulations. I'm sure a few of the

females will be disappointed."

When Daniel looked at Phillip, it looked as if he were a little disappointed, as well.

"Thanks." It was the only response he could come up with at the moment.

"See you tomorrow. Meeting about the club campaign at ten thirty."

"Right."

Phillip knocked on the frame of the door before he left.

Daniel let out a deep breath. The plan seemed to work so far. He hoped his luck would           hold           out.

# Melting the Snow

# Chapter Three

CiCi was nervous. She wasn't sure her dark, skinny jeans and chocolate-colored sweater with her knee high brown boots was her best casual outfit. After changing three times, she'd ended up wearing the outfit she had on in the first place. In all of her twenty-seven years, she could not remember putting so much effort into her appearance to attract a specific man.

The front door of Villanova's opened, and she realized it was too late to worry any longer. *He* had entered the building.

The illusive *He* noticed her right away and held up a finger, signaling he would get a drink and be right over. She continued to take deep breaths until he came over to join her. He took off his coat and made himself comfortable in the chair across from her.

"No rushing off today?"

"No." He sipped his drink and sighed. "I don't have any meetings until mid-morning, so I have a little extra time. What about you? No portfolio today?"

"No. I had a meeting yesterday, but the project is basically finished, so I have a couple weeks off." She took a long, luxurious sip from her own cup.

He smiled and nodded. "With all this free time on your hands, I suppose having coffee with strange men is out of the question?"

The introduction she had been dreading. As soon as he heard her last name, either the dollar signs would glow in his eyes, or he would run away from the lady who wrote children's books for a living. Maybe it was time to try something different.

"I'm CiCi. And you are?"

His Adam's apple bounced when he swallowed. "Daniel."

"Okay, Daniel. Now we're not strangers."

He smiled. "CiCi. Not strangers now. Might I be so bold as to ask what you might be doing with all this free time?"

"Besides meeting you for peppermint mochas?" she asked with a mischievous twinkle in her eye.

"Well, that's a given at this point," he said with a dimpled grin.

"Maybe see a show. There is an exhibit at the Natural History Museum I wanted to check out." He raised an eyebrow at her answer. "Or I've heard about this roller derby tournament this weekend. Maybe do a little Christmas shopping. Oh, and I've been invited to a club opening. I might drop by."

"Roller derby sounds promising." He laughed before taking another sip.

CiCi's heart fluttered, and her stomach flipped at the melodious sound. She knew it was the beginning of a beautiful friendship.

~*~*~

"Are you going to explain why every female I've run into is asking me if you're married?" His personal assistant extraordinaire plopped herself down in the chair in front of Daniel's desk.

"You've gotta back me up on this. I know it might seem crazy, but I think this is the one way to keep the ladies away at work. What have you been saying?"

Samantha shook her head full of auburn waves and rolled her bright blue eyes. "That you keep your personal life private."

"Thank you, Samantha. I can't take a chance that . . ." His throat closed up when he thought about his last job. The memory of the daily comments about his physique, the touching that wasn't always so innocent, and the way it all ended raised his blood pressure in an instant.

"I know, so I'll have your back on this one." Samantha gave him a sympathetic smile; she knew how hard it was for him to work with all the unwanted attention. He was thankful that she wasn't ten years younger and unmarried, or she might have been part of the problem. Instead, she made it clear that he shouldn't have to deal with unwanted attention just because he was twenty-eight and in his prime. As a friend, she always did whatever she could to make this job easier on him.

"Knock, knock."

Both Samantha and Daniel directed their attention to the woman in Daniel's doorway.

"Miss Westcott, what can I do for you?" Daniel asked in his politest tone.

"I had a few more questions for you if you can spare a moment." The smile that was plastered on her face was saccharine sweet and completely fake.

"I'll be at my desk if you need me." Samantha excused herself, but Daniel was confident she would be keeping tabs on his visitor.

"What were your questions, Miss Westcott?" Daniel motioned for her to sit.

"Please, call me Simone." She took the seat Samantha had vacated.

"Simone," he repeated.

"Yes, well. I was wondering about the opening of Chameleon. All of us on the account are invited with a plus one. Will your wife be coming with you?"

Daniel cringed. He knew a fishing expedition when he heard one. "I will have to check her schedule."

"I'll leave it open. Just let me know when you find out." Simone stood and smoothed out her skirt, which looked rather tight on her slightly curved form.

"Sure thing." His phone rang, saving him from furthering the conversation. "If there's nothing else . . ."

She shook her head. "No. I'll see myself out."

He nodded and answered the phone. "Daniel Digby."

"You need rescuing?" Samantha asked in a whisper.

"Just finishing." Simone waved at him before shutting his office door. "Please keep an eye out for that one. She was asking about my plus one for the club opening."

"I'll do my best." They both laughed before they ended their call.

Samantha pulled out a little notebook from her desk drawer. She opened it to a list of names and added one more in red, capitalized letters: SIMONE WESTCOTT.

# Melting the Snow

# *Chapter Four*

On their third meeting, Daniel and CiCi began to let the walls they had built around themselves crumble, bit by bit.

Their sixth meeting was on a Saturday. Since Daniel didn't have any work commitments, he'd asked if CiCi wouldn't mind bundling up and going ice-skating at Rockefeller Center. By the end of the afternoon, they were huddled together with two cups of hot chocolate without any awkwardness.

Their seventh meeting came late on a Sunday morning, followed by brunch and a matinee movie of the original version of *Miracle on 34th Street*. CiCi even got Daniel to admit he still wrote letters to Santa every year as part of his family's tradition.

By their eighth meeting, Daniel could officially admit to himself that he had found the one woman in New York with whom he could be himself. Two things still hadn't been discussed: their last names and their exact occupations.

Meeting number ten was the Wednesday before Thanksgiving, which meant they would not be seeing each other for at least two days.

"Your niece is flying in tonight?" Daniel asked before sipping his coffee.

"Yes. Her husband and son are coming

with her. I know it sounds weird that my niece is married with a child while I'm . . . not." CiCi closed her eyes and took a deep breath.

"I take it she's much older than I would imagine." Daniel scooted to sit on the edge of his seat and took her hand.

CiCi gave him a soft smile and looked into his eyes. "My older sister, Bridgett, is actually my half-sister. She was nineteen when I was born, and she married my brother-in-law after my first birthday. My niece, Emily, came not long after. My family is a little hard to explain, and I don't get to see them much."

"I get it." Daniel gave her hand a squeeze. "I'm off to my parents tomorrow. I see them all the time, but every time is memorable."

"At least I can meet you here Saturday morning for a little while."

Daniel smiled, but it didn't quite make it to his eyes. "Yes." He closed his lids and contemplated what he wanted to say. Could he tell her he physically ached during the hours they were apart? Would she believe him if he told her he'd never felt so close to someone so fast? Did she want to know he was falling in love with her even though he didn't know her last name?

CiCi lifted her hand and placed it on his cheek. His eyes fluttered open and met hers.

"I will miss you, too," she whispered.

His smile brightened, and he turned his

head to kiss her palm.

She returned her hand to where he had held it a moment before on his thigh.

"Saturday?" he asked.

She gave him a timid nod. "Saturday."

~*~*~

"Marcy, this is amazing!" Emily gushed before she took another bite of the roasted turkey.

"Reggie helped." Marcy directed her gaze to her husband, who sat across the table from her. "But only a little."

"Hey," the handsome butler objected. "I injected the bird with my special spices before you put it in a pan and threw it in the oven."

CiCi laughed with Emily, Emily's husband, James, and Marcy. There was always a debate over who was the best chef in the household. Holidays were when the competition was the fiercest.

CiCi remembered the last Thanksgiving she had spent with her mother. They had known she didn't have much time left and made sure it was the best the Newport family ever had. CiCi had tried to duplicate that feeling in the years since, but this year was the closest she had come.

This year, she had Emily, James, and little Jamie to celebrate with her, Marcy, and

Reggie. Her career was at an all-time high. Last, but by no means least, she was falling in love. She had so much for which to be thankful.

"No. Please, no," James groaned.

CiCi brought herself back into the conversation. "What?"

"I was thinking of doing a little Black Friday shopping," Emily said with faux enthusiasm.

"The deals are much better online this year." CiCi knew none of them wanted to brave the stores on Black Friday. She had a much better idea. "Let's pull out the laptop first thing and get what we can. Then tomorrow night I'll take you and James with me to the opening of Marco's club."

"Marco St. Croix?" Emily asked with more excitement than CiCi would have expected.

"Yes, but I knew him when he was little Marco who cut my hair in the first grade, so I got an invite." CiCi snickered at how the boy who'd cut her hair had become New York City's leading club owner.

"I'm up for it," James added. "It's called Chameleon, right?"

"Yes, the club's theme changes every night of the week. Marco said this is the VIP night and they are doing a Southern Blues theme." CiCi was rather excited about the outing. It wasn't some stuffy charity event where she would have to be on her best behavior. She might enjoy herself for a change.

"Reggie and I will watch Jamie," Marcy offered.

"You're sure?" Emily asked.

"We'd love to," Reggie answered. "Please, take her out. She's become such a homebody lately."

"Except for her coffee dates," Marcy added before sipping her wine.

"Dates?" Emily raised her eyebrow in question. "Did you meet someone?"

"It's new. We've been meeting for coffee; that's it." CiCi took another bite of the scrumptious turkey.

"Okay, we'll go if I can get the details on this mystery guy."

CiCi gave Emily her signature hard stare, but after a few seconds, she gave in. "Fine."

~*~*~

Being the only unmarried Digby child, Daniel was used to all the jeers about his love life. Even after the horrible year with the sexual harassment suit, it seemed this occasion was no different.

"Any hot women at this new job, Danny Boy?" Daniel's eldest brother, Jeff, asked while wiggling his brow.

Daniel shook his head while his father laughed and slapped Jeff on the back. He looked to his mother and caught a sympathetic glance.

"I'm not looking for anything like that. Especially not at work." He took another swig from the beer he had been nursing for the last hour while they watched football.

"So, you getting it somewhere else?" his father asked. "Millie! Danny's got a lady."

"Stew," Millie admonished her husband. "Leave him alone."

"What? He's got the Digby looks. No wonder them ladies are begging at his door."

Daniel was teetering on the edge of a Hulk-like meltdown. His father and brothers used their good looks to their full advantage. Daniel always wanted to earn his way in the world instead of flirting his way to the top. Jeff was the publisher of a popular car magazine, and their other two brothers, Hank and Bruce, worked for him. It was always hot cars and hotter women with them. All three of their wives could have been mistaken for Victoria's Secret models.

His twin sister, Daisy, was the only normal one of the bunch. She was a stay-at-home mother with twin three-year-old girls while her husband, Kip, worked as an insurance agent.

Thankfully, she came in at that moment and gave him her signature calming smile.

"Dad, leave Daniel alone. That woman was stalking him." Daisy sat on the arm of

Daniel's recliner. "Give them something," she whispered. "They're not going to stop, and you know it." She slipped her arm around him.

"I did meet someone," Daniel announced.

An instant hush fell over the room, and his mother muted the television.

"Where?" Millie asked with hope in her light tone.

"The coffee shop near my new place." He shrugged his shoulders.

"You should have us over for a housewarming and invite her. I can make my lemon Bundt cake. Everyone loves my Bundt cake."

"We just met. It's still new." Daniel chugged the rest of his lukewarm beer.

"When he's ready," Daisy emphasized each word, "he will invite us over."

"Thank you." Daniel wrapped his arm around his sister's waist and gave her a hug.

"Just make sure I meet her first." She lifted her arm from his shoulder and raked her fingers through his hair. "She has to know part of this family is, in fact, sane."

Daniel smiled and hugged her tighter. He *really* loved his sister.

# Melting the Snow

# Chapter Five

Even in the depths of the frostbitten evening of November, Daniel had rivulets of sweat trailing down his spine. His nerves hadn't taken such a death grip on him since he had started out in the business. The opening night at Chameleon was his first big event for Henderson PR, and he was scared shitless.

He went through his mental checklist while he walked among the club goers. Everything seemed to be going as planned until he spotted Simone walking toward him. His instincts made him bring his left thumb up underneath his left ring finger to feel for the band he'd been wearing for weeks. Panic surged through him when he noticed it wasn't there. An image of the silver band sitting beside his bathroom sink hit him hard before he shoved his hand deep in his pocket.

"Everything looks wonderful," Simone gushed before giving him a kiss on the cheek.

"Yes, Marco seems happy with it." He looked to the VIP section, which was situated above and to the side of the dance floor and where the owner of Chameleon was holding court.

"Little wife at home?" Simone asked while her fingertips slid across his bicep to his forearm.

"No." He coughed out and jerked his arm away. "Um, she's supposed to meet up with me later."

"I'd love to meet her. Come find me if she shows." Simone licked her lips and gave him a once-over before she sauntered off.

He blew out a deep breath. Hopefully he could finish his duties and head out early.

One final check, and he would be free. That was when Marco caught his attention and motioned for him to come to the VIP section. Daniel psyched himself up for the feedback in store for him while he made his way to Marco.

"This is amazing, Marco," Daniel commented when he shook Marco's hand.

"I love how this overlooks the whole club. You get the whole experience." Marco smiled at his surroundings.

Marco was young but smart. His head for numbers and uncanny ability to book unbelievable talent brought him quickly to his current position. The six foot three man stood a little above Daniel, but he came nowhere close to matching him in the looks department. He had unfortunately inherited his mother's large nose, but his natural dark skin, almond colored eyes, and trim build made up for most of it.

Marco stood a bit straighter when he noticed a green-eyed beauty on the dance floor. "CiCi!" he called to her.

Daniel froze at the sound of her name. He directed his eyes to the woman Marco was calling. It couldn't be her. His mind raced over the guest list, and he couldn't recall anyone named CiCi on it.

One look and he was positive it was she. CiCi's arms rested on a man's shoulders while his hands rested on her hips. Daniel's hair stood on end as jealousy swiftly ran through him. He turned away when Marco yelled her name again, praying she wouldn't notice him.

CiCi noticed Marco and waved at him. He motioned for her to come to the VIP area, and she gave him a thumbs-up signal and leaned in to whisper to her dance partner.

"You're going to love CiCi. I've known her most my life." Marco let out a nervous laugh.

Daniel immediately surmised Marco had eyes for the fair CiCi. There was no way this conversation would go well.

"Marco!" CiCi rushed and hugged her friend tight while the man she was dancing with and another woman came up behind her.

"How you doing, hun?" Marco asked before kissing her cheek.

"Oh, you know." CiCi looked to Marco's side and noticed who was standing there. "Daniel." His name escaped her in a surprised whisper. "I wasn't expecting to see you tonight."

He recognized her smile, the one that graced her face every time he would walk into *their* coffee shop.

"I suppose I should have asked which club opening you were going to, huh?" Daniel smiled, and then turned his attention to the two other people in the group.

"Marco, you remember my niece, Emily, and her husband, James?"

"It's a great honor to be here," Emily gushed when she shook Marco's hand.

"You've got a great place here. Thanks for letting us tag along with CiCi," James said with a grin.

"Not a problem at all," Marco responded as he noticed Daniel and CiCi lost in one another. "Why don't you all have a seat? I'll have them deliver a bottle of champagne." Marco motioned to a seating area nearby.

Daniel's heart soared when CiCi nodded and took his hand. He couldn't believe, of all the places in New York City, he would bump into her there.

Once they got settled, Emily began to fire off the questions. "How do the two of you know each other?"

Daniel spoke before CiCi had the chance. "We met at this coffee place we both like. It seems we are there at the same time every day, so we started drinking our coffee together."

Emily let out a soft squeak before James

could grab her hand to calm her. "You're the one?"

"The one?" Daniel eyed CiCi and noticed a red tinge to her cheeks.

"I told them about meeting you yesterday." CiCi answered and tried to change the subject. "How was your Thanksgiving?"

"Same old, same old. I only made it through without strangling one of my brothers because my sister talked me down." He laughed, remembering that Daisy wanted to meet CiCi. Now here he was, meeting her family first. "Are you two having a nice trip? CiCi mentioned you were coming in from L. A."

"It's been wonderful," James said while he put his arm around his wife's shoulders. "CiCi has been a great hostess."

Soon enough, a server came over with a bottle of champagne with Marco's compliments. The four drank and talked, getting a bit tipsy. Marco joined them for awhile. Before he was called away by some other friends, he gave CiCi another hug and a look of approval for Daniel.

"We have to dance." CiCi took Daniel's hand, and he followed her down the stairs onto the dance floor.

Daniel was willing to do anything that brought him closer to CiCi. He slipped his hands around her waist when her arms wrapped around his neck.

"I've wanted to get you like this all night," she whispered in his ear before threading her fingers through the hair at the nape of his neck.

"God," he groaned. His pants grew tight at the feel of her body pulsating against his own. "Do you have any idea what you're doing to me?"

"The same thing you're doing to me?" she asked with a slight smirk.

He drew his fingertips up her torso and grasped her elbow, bringing her hand down to rest on his hip. The feeling of her fluttering pulse against his palm where he rested it on her neck sped up his own. When her tongue peeked out from between her lips, he knew what she was waiting for.

The music swelled around them while he dipped his head. The feel of her lips caressing his made him forget where he was. His heart twisted in his chest. Their lips and tongues danced to the erotic sounds from the guitar on stage. The couple lost themselves in each other and the music. Nothing else existed.

The kiss came to a slow ending with a few soft pecks. CiCi wrapped her arms around Daniel's neck and rested her forehead on his shoulder. He was brought back into his surroundings. His focus caught a swath of red. Simone. "Shit!" he whispered.

"What?" CiCi pulled away and looked at

him with a shocked expression.

"Not you. No, nothing about you." Daniel swallowed hard when he saw Simone trying to work her way through the crowd towards them. "You wanna get out of here?"

His nervousness confused her, but after the kiss they had shared, her hormones were on high alert and ready for more. "Yeah."

The next instant, Daniel was weaving his way toward the entrance of the club. The couple made it to the coatroom with Simone trailing behind. Daniel pulled CiCi inside to hide and made a plea to the coat check attendant to help them out.

"Excuse me." Simone's voice echoed through the room and brought the attendant's attention to her. Daniel pressed his finger to CiCi's lips to keep her quiet.

"Yes, ma'am?" the attendant asked.

"Did you see a couple come through here? He's tall, dark hair, and green eyes. She's a curvy thing with brown hair."

"Um." The attendant squinted her eyes while she thought. "I saw them, but they turned around before they got to the door. Maybe they forgot something inside."

"Maybe." Simone looked the girl over, and then rolled her eyes and went into the main area.

"Thank you," Daniel told the attendant while he dug his ticket out of his pocket.

"No problem," she replied and took their

tickets.

"Do I get to know what that was about?" He could see that CiCi was a tad annoyed about being hidden in the coatroom.

"I work with her, and she's been a complete nightmare. I'm not really sure what her problem is." He snuck a quick peck. "Forgive me?"

"Fine. Where are you taking me?"

"My place. You can text Emily the address so she'll know where you'll be." He hoped that the time they had spent together in the last few weeks would make her comfortable with the idea of coming home with him.

"Okay."

That one small word spoke volumes. She trusted him, and he would make sure he kept her trust.

The attendant brought them their coats, and with a quick thank you, they were out the door and into a cab.

# Chapter Six

CiCi was relieved when they pulled up to a brownstone that had been converted into apartments only ten blocks away from her own home.

Once inside, Daniel told her to text Emily his address while they rode the elevator to his apartment. Not ten seconds later, Emily texted with a warning to remember to use a condom.

CiCi laughed, and Daniel caught sight of the text.

He wrapped his arms around her waist from behind. "I was hoping you'd share a drink with me, but if you're interested in taking things further . . ."

Her face heated at the thought of his lips discovering the rest of her body while he began to kiss the side of her neck.

"How about a drink first?"

"Of course," he answered when the elevator stopped at his floor.

They were in his apartment with their coats off within a minute. She instantly fell in love with the place. It was a loft style apartment that looked like a comfortable bachelor pad. A chocolate brown couch with large cushions sat in his living room area in front of a flat screen TV. A queen-sized bed was made up with a dark blue comforter in his bedroom area. What she loved the most was the small Christmas tree decorated in silver and blue standing on a corner table. He reclaimed her attention when his hand found hers and led her through the dining area into his small kitchen.

Daniel picked her up and set her on the butcher-block kitchen island, then gave her a soft kiss. "I'm not a big beer drinker, but I do have some apple ale, if you're interested. I always have some on hand during the holidays." He opened his refrigerator and pulled out two green glass bottles.

She smiled when she caught a glimpse of the familiar label. "I love this brand. Reggie got me hooked a few years ago."

"Reggie?" he questioned before handing her an open bottle.

She thought quickly. "He's kind of a surrogate father. My dad passed away when I was sixteen, and Reggie stepped in."

"So I don't have any competition?" He raised his eyebrow and moved to stand between her thighs.

"No." CiCi ran her fingertip across his clean-shaven jawline. "I haven't been interested in anyone in a long time."

Daniel placed his hand on her hip, his thumb caressing her through the thin material of her shirt. "I haven't, either. If this is heading where I think it is, you should know I haven't done . . . *it* in a long time."

"Really?" She understood why someone in her situation would abstain, but she couldn't believe a guy as gorgeous as Daniel hadn't had women more than willing to take a tumble in his bed.

He concentrated his gaze on where his thumb was moving across her hip. "I've had problems with . . . unwanted attention. I haven't felt enough of a connection with someone to go further." He lifted his chin to look in her eyes. "Not until you, anyway."

CiCi took the bottle from his hand and placed it next to hers. She moved her body forward a little bit so she could wrap her legs around his waist. If she wanted things to go further, she knew the moment to take a little initiative had arrived. "I think this is the part when you show me your bedroom."

Daniel lifted her off the island and held her close. His eyes stayed on hers while he took the twenty or so steps to his bedroom area. She bounced a little when he set her on the bed.

"Before we get any further, I need to check something." Daniel opened his bedside table drawer. "Every birthday since I turned fifteen, one of my brothers has given me a box." He pulled out an unopened box of magnum-sized condoms and checked the expiration date on the side of the box to confirm they were still good. "My college girlfriend bumped into my oldest brother at a party. She was flirting with him, and one thing led to another. I guess when it came time for the big event, she began laughing hysterically."

"What?" CiCi giggled. "Why?"

"I guess she told him she thought he would be as big as I was. According to her, he didn't measure up. People started talking, and my other brothers found out. The next birthday, they started giving me the magnums."

She couldn't help but look at the noticeable bulge in his jeans. A little moan left her. The thought of anything bigger than the five-inchers she'd experienced in the past got her a little wet.

Daniel set the box on the bedside table before he sat next to her on the bed. "It is something I'm kind of self-conscious about, hence this conversation."

CiCi tried not to laugh at his obvious discomfort. "You think I might not be satisfied because you're too big?"

"Um . . ." He squeezed his eyes shut tight and scratched at his forehead. "It usually goes one of two ways."

"And those are?" she asked while she took his hand, hoping to reassure him.

"Either they are too scared to come near it, or they can't get enough."

CiCi brought her hand to his jaw and turned his head to look at her. "Why don't you let me judge for myself." With a slight lean, her lips met his.

Their kiss continued while she coaxed him to lie on his back. She sat on his thighs and began to unbutton his shirt. One by one, each button left a hole, and her fingers caressed his exposed chest. Once the last button was undone, he sat up a bit and took it completely off.

"May I?" he asked when he pulled at the hem of her silk tank blouse.

"You may."

He lifted the material up her torso and over her head, revealing her breasts encased in ivory lace. CiCi moved her hands behind her back and unhooked her bra.

"Daniel?" she asked while she caressed his jaw.

"Yes?" He moved his gaze to her eyes.

"I'm going to get up and take off the rest."

"Okay."

He couldn't believe she was so calm. His pulse was racing and he was the hardest he'd been in his life. This part had never been slow with him, always fast and frantic. Not with CiCi. Every movement was deliberate, each touch gentle.

He was brought back to the moment when he noticed the beautiful, naked woman taking off his shoes and socks. Once she had completed that task, she crawled into his lap.

"You're not saying anything. Is this

okay?"

He could sense her pulling back as she crossed her arms over her chest. It was time to confess a little bit more.

"It's fine, more than fine." He uncrossed her arms and pulled her into his own. The feel of her bare breasts against his chest was a thrill he wouldn't soon forget. "I'm not used to the slow approach. I have to say though, I like it very much." He kissed her softly.

"Good," she mumbled against his lips. "I'm trying my best not to be nervous, so slow is the only speed I can go at right now." She trailed her fingers across his chest to his happy trail. Once she reached the button on his jeans, she stopped. "Ready?"

"For you, yes." He slid his hands underneath her and stood; then he set her down to stand in front of him.

Her fingers unbuttoned and unzipped his jeans to reveal soft, green cotton underneath. Without another moment's hesitation, she moved a hand to each hip and skimmed both articles of clothing down along his toned legs to his feet.

He stepped out of both and tossed them aside with his foot. She began to trail kisses up his calf with her head cast down. Once she got to his knee, she switched to his other calf and repeated her kisses. CiCi kept her eyes closed and avoided the hard-on protruding from between his legs. Her index finger caressed the large vein from base to tip. His soft moan brought her gaze to meet his.

CiCi stood and placed her hands on his chest; his hands lay on her hips.

"Daniel, I could never be scared. You're magnificent."

"I would say you're fairly magnificent yourself." His fingertips trailed across the soft, smooth skin of her hip.

"Then we should be better together." She pushed him to lie on the bed, then she climbed on and lay beside him.

Daniel turned them so they were on their sides facing each other. Their lips and hands began exploring. He rubbed himself against her center and could feel the wetness coating her thighs.

"The box," she whispered before she continued to kiss the side of his neck.

Flinging his hand behind him, he grabbed the box of condoms from his nightstand. He had it opened and a packet out in no time at all.

"Let me." She took the packet from him and rolled him on his back.

He watched in fascination as his erection stood tall in anticipation of her touch. She rolled it to the base and pinching the tip. A groan erupted from his chest at the sight.

"That has to be one of the sexiest things I have ever seen." He crooked his finger, beckoning her for a kiss.

They shared one slow, sensual kiss before he flipped her on her back and nestled himself between her thighs. He rubbed the tip across her clit, making her nipples pebble while she moaned.

His gaze met hers, and she nodded her approval. Her eyes never left his while he pressed forward. Slow, shallow thrusts allowed her to easily adjust to his size. She wrapped her legs around his waist and circled her hips to help him go deeper.

They established a slow, powerful rhythm, something he had never experienced before. His chest brushed across her nipples as he rested his weight on his forearms. She pulled his head down to kiss him and squeezed her thighs tighter. Their pace never faltered, slowly building toward a release they had both waited so long for.

"Daniel," she whispered. Her walls began to tremble around him.

He groaned in response as he began to reach his peak. Several deep thrusts had her quivering and panting in ecstasy. Daniel followed with a few quick movements and a deep moan.

His lips met hers when he slipped out of her. "Let me take care of this." He rolled onto his back to remove the condom and put it in the trashcan beside his bed.

CiCi curled up next to him, her head

resting on his chest.

"I'm not sure what the protocol is here," he said while his fingers threaded through her hair.

"Protocol?"

"You know, what to say after the best sex of your life. I'll start with thank you."

She kissed across his chest before moving to his lips. "Believe me, the pleasure was all mine."

~*~*~

CiCi woke the next morning to an arm around her waist and an erection nestled between her butt cheeks.

"Morning," she sighed when she shimmied against him.

"Mmmmm," Daniel groaned.

A few feather light kisses on her shoulder and a brush of his fingers across her breast, and she was ready to go once more.

"Need you," she whispered while she pushed her backside against him.

"Like this?"

She took him to mean on their sides with him behind her. "God, yes."

He moved away for a moment to grab a condom and roll it on. She felt him lift her leg and move it to drape over his own. Then he was there, between her thighs and finding his way inside.

His pace was slow and languid, but his finger caressing her clit made her reach bliss quicker than the night before. The feeling coupled with his whispers and moans in her ear sent her over the edge.

Their euphoria was short-lived; CiCi's phone began blasting Emily's ringtone.

"Oh, hell. It's Emily."

"It's fine. Get it while I clean up." Daniel kissed her shoulder before getting out of bed and going into the bathroom.

"Hello?"

"I left you alone for as long as I could. It's already nine, and we have to be at the luncheon by eleven."

"Shit!" CiCi jumped out of bed, frantically gathering her clothes. "Can you get my burgundy dress out with my black boots? I can be there in about thirty minutes."

"Sure. I want the whole story when you get here."

"Fine. See you soon." She ended the call, threw the phone on the bed, and began to get dressed.

"I guess a shower together would be too much to hope for?"

Her breath caught in her throat when she saw Daniel standing in the bathroom doorway with only a towel wrapped around his waist.

"Sorry, I've got a lunch thing in less than two hours." She didn't want to tell him about the speech she would be making or all the photos that might be in the paper the next day.

"Okay, I will let you go on two conditions." He moved over to her while she finished dressing.

"Two conditions, huh?"

Daniel nodded. "One, I need your phone number."

She grabbed her phone from the bed and handed it to him. "Just dial your number from my phone, and you'll have it."

"Two." He dialed his number and heard his phone ringing before he ended the call. "I need to know when I can see you again."

"I'll be tied up all day today, and Emily and James are leaving tomorrow. So it won't be until Monday."

"Then we'll meet for coffee at eight and talk about what happens next?" he asked.

"More like last night and this morning, I hope." CiCi gave him a kiss she hoped would tide him over until Monday.

"You can count on that." He walked her over to the door and gave her another kiss. "Monday?"

"Can't wait."

# Melting the Snow

# *Chapter Seven*

CiCi sat impatiently waiting in her favorite chair at Villanova Coffee. She was early, but she couldn't help herself. The last two days had been both wonderful and awful. Wonderful because she could text and talk with the man she felt safe calling her boyfriend. Awful because she was dreading telling him the truth.

She sipped from her favorite drink, then turned her head when she heard the door open.

"You're early," Daniel sighed in relief before he walked over to her, ridding himself of his gloves and coat as he went.

"I told you I couldn't wait."

He dumped his things in the chair across from hers before grabbing her hands and pulling her into his arms. "I missed you."

"I missed you too," she laughed, but before she could take another breath, his lips were on hers.

They pulled apart when they heard a not-so-subtle clearing throat.

"Sorry," Daniel said when he turned to the person to apologize for their public display. He paled at the sight of the woman standing before them. "Simone. What a surprise."

"Yes, I saw you duck in here and thought

we might have some coffee before work. I see I interrupted your date with the Missus." Simone fixed a wide smile on her face before she offered her hand to CiCi. "I must have missed you the other night at the club. I'm Simone Westcott. I work with Daniel."

CiCi shook her hand in somewhat of a haze of confusion. *Missus?* "Yes, well . . . We kind of rushed out of there. Sorry about that."

Daniel had to think fast before everything imploded. "We were having a coffee before I head into the office."

"Why don't you bring Mrs. Digby into the office and show her around." Simone turned her attention to CiCi. "You look so familiar. Have we met before?"

"I don't think so." CiCi faced Daniel with confusion. "Am I missing something?"

Daniel took her hand and brought it to his lips. "I know we haven't announced it, but I couldn't keep it from the people at work. I wore my ring the first day, and they all noticed. I'm sorry I didn't tell you. Please forgive me."

CiCi could see his plea in his eyes. *Please go along with this, and I swear I will explain it all later.*

"Oh, my," Simone said in shock. "You're CiCi Newport."

"Guilty." CiCi gave Simone a weak smile while she slipped her arm around Daniel's waist in a show of support.

Daniel stiffened in her arms, and CiCi knew he'd realized she was Winston Newport's billionaire daughter.

"Well, I guess it would be Digby now." Simone let out a dry laugh.

"She hasn't officially changed it." Daniel squeezed nervously at CiCi's hip below his hand.

"Now that the cat's out of the bag, so to speak, why don't we all share a cab to the office and you can show your lovely bride around?" Simone raised her brow as if to challenge Daniel.

"Um," Daniel began to object but was cut off.

"Let me grab my coffee, and we can go." Simone moved over to the counter to order.

Daniel grabbed both of CiCi's hands. "Please, please, don't hate me. If you go along with me on this, once we get to my office I will explain everything."

"You want me to pretend I'm your wife?" she whispered with a strong edge of anger. "Are you married?"

"No! God, no. I just had to say I was." He squeezed her hands in his. "Please help me."

CiCi knew she needed to get in touch with her therapist, because following through with his plan made her certifiable. "Okay, but it better be good . . . Mr. Digby, is it?"

"Yes, Miss Newport." He leaned in and

caressed her lips with his. "Thank you."

~*~*~

The cab ride was tense at best. Simone launched into a story about what they had missed after they left the club on Friday night. Neither Daniel nor CiCi heard much of what she was saying. They were each focused on what might happen when they arrived at Daniel's workplace.

*I don't even know where he works.*

Simone paid the cab driver and ushered them out. They were in the elevator, riding upward before CiCi could get her bearings.

They reached the thirty-fifth floor, and the elevator doors opened to show the large Henderson Public Relations logo on the wall. CiCi froze.

"Come on. We'll go straight to my office."

"I can't go in there," she whispered in panic.

"You said you —"

"Ah, Daniel. I need to move our meeting to this afternoon." Daniel's boss, Phillip, greeted him while CiCi inched out of the elevator. "CiCi?"

"Hello, Phillip. So nice to see you."

Phillip leaned in and gave CiCi a kiss on the cheek.

"You know Daniel's wife?" Simone asked Phillip casually.

"Wife?" He looked to Daniel, who confirmed it with a slight nod. "Well, this makes things interesting."

"It won't be a problem, will it, Phillip? I swear I didn't know anything about the marketing changes until a few weeks ago." CiCi hoped Daniel wouldn't get in trouble for being 'married' to a client.

"I don't see why it would be. He's not representing you. I told Lori I would handle you personally." Phillip smiled at one of his newest clients.

Daniel scratched at his forehead, a nervous habit he couldn't seem to break. He needed to focus on getting them to his office.

"Great, we were a bit worried," Daniel uttered before he put his arm around CiCi's waist. "Well, I'm going to show CiCi around. I will catch up with you this afternoon."

Phillip nodded. "Two o'clock."

"Got it." Daniel ushered CiCi down the hallway.

They made it to his office to find Samantha at her desk.

"Good morning, boss."

"Samantha, this is my wife, CiCi. Hug her and pretend you're great friends." Down the hall, Simone was walking around the corner.

Recognition passing over her face, Samantha got up from her desk and hugged CiCi. "Don't worry. He really is a great guy," she assured.

"God, I hope so." CiCi let out a deep breath when she released Samantha.

"Hold my calls." Daniel opened his office door and let CiCi in.

The door clicked shut behind him, and she sat on his couch.

"This is not how I saw this morning going." Daniel sat next to her and put his head in his hands.

"Me, either." CiCi tried to take a few deep, cleansing breaths to calm herself.

"God, I don't know where to start." He rubbed the heels of his hands into his eye sockets.

"Let me see if I'm on the right track here." She began to count on her fingers. "You work for the firm where I am a client. You're not handling my account, so no harm done there. But for some reason, your colleagues believe you are married. How am I doing so far?"

"Yes, yes, and yes." Daniel turned to look at her. "I swear I have a good explanation for all of it."

"Let's have it."

He let out a long breath and launched into his story.

"I did an internship with Stanley Brothers PR my senior year in college. I had been dating my girlfriend, Missy, for about two years at the time. They offered me a full time position when I graduated. Missy was livid. She thought every woman working there was after me and gave me an ultimatum. I chose the job, but it turns out she was kind of right."

"That must have sucked." She unconsciously began running her hand up and down his spine.

"Yeah. I was the only guy in my department, and everyday at least one of them would do something to make me feel uncomfortable. After a while, I couldn't take it any longer. I quit and went to work for Martling and Martling. Things were great for a few years. I got promoted with my own office and inherited Samantha from the man I took over for."

"New job, promotion, and Samantha. I take it something must have happened for you to leave?"

He rubbed his chest with the tips of his fingers as though he were soothing a deep ache. "They brought in a new V. P. after I'd been there about three years: Lena Holland."

"I've heard of her. She's quite an ice princess, if the rumors are true."

"Yes, what Lena wanted, Lena got. The fact she was fifteen years older than me didn't stop her from setting her sights on me."

"Oh, wow." CiCi could imagine the intimidating glamazon she had seen at several events lording over Daniel.

"For a while, it was all about touching me

whenever we were in the same room. It was uncomfortable but bearable, since every other aspect of the job was pretty perfect. About six months ago, she amped things up. She set up a meeting that the client mysteriously canceled so it was just the two of us at some five-star restaurant. At one point, she tried to get me to take a trip to Boston with her for a fundraiser with a national charity we were trying to land. I thank God everyday my brother, Bruce, decided to get married that weekend and flew the whole family to the Bahamas."

"Did you talk to anybody about it?"

He looked over to his office door and smiled. "Yes, Samantha knew everything. Being the amazing personal assistant she is, she kept track of dates, times, and everything I never thought about. It all came in handy when I needed it."

CiCi could feel the worst part of his story approaching and took his hand. She laced their fingers together and looked him in the eye. "I'm still here. Keep going."

"I met Phillip Reese two years ago, and he'd tried to convince me to come work here every time we ran into each other since. Three months ago, I told him I was ready to talk. My contract with M and M was up for negotiation, and I couldn't stand the thought of committing myself any longer. I told Phillip I would take this job, and I was getting ready to put in my notice.

"While I was trying to do everything I could to tie up all my accounts, I spent one night on my office couch. Lena got a key to my office and came in the next morning." He squeezed CiCi's hand and turned his focus out the window across from them. "When I woke up, she had *me* in her hand and was about to get on top. Once I realized what was happening, I threw her off and ran to the other side of my office. Samantha rushed in once she heard the commotion and figured out exactly what was going on. Lena started yelling for Samantha to get out, but she knew better and asked me what I wanted her to do."

"I hope you told her to call the police."

"Close. Security. I barricaded myself in the corner of my office while Lena ranted, sans pants. I held it together until they removed her from my office, then puked into my office trashcan for about ten minutes. The company let me out of my contract, and we settled a sexual harassment suit a few weeks later."

"I can't imagine going through something like that." CiCi scooted close enough to him to lay her head on his shoulder. "Friday night was the first time you'd done anything since it happened?"

Daniel nodded and closed his eyes. "After Missy and all these women coming onto me, sexually aggressive women turn me off. The few women I have tried to date were so far at the other end of the spectrum, I ended up scaring them away. So when my friend, Gabe, suggested I pretend to be married, I thought it wasn't a half bad idea." He opened his eyes and laid his cheek against the top of her head. "Everyone has seemed to respect the ring, except Simone. It's weird, though, because she has wanted to meet my wife since the day I started here."

"How will this all work? The press will have a field day if they catch wind of it."

"I hadn't thought of that." Daniel turned so they were facing each other and held her hands in his. "I know this is such an utter fuck up, but I panicked. I'll walk into Phillip's office right now and confess if you want me to."

CiCi could see the pain radiating in his eyes. A man so amazing didn't deserve what had been thrown at him. Earlier in the day, she had been thinking of a few years down the road. His razor would sit in the shower next to hers. Maybe a nursery would take over the office beside their room.

"If we can keep it between us and Phillip, I think it could work."

"Yes, of course. I will talk to Phillip this afternoon and make sure he keeps things to himself."

"What about Simone?" She was worried

about another female viper causing destruction in his life.

"I will talk to her when I talk to Phillip. Hopefully, she will see she has to agree with the boss."

CiCi leaned in and kissed him softly. "As long as you're okay with having a billionaire wife."

"Yes, it was a bit of a shock, but I think we can work something out." Daniel smiled before giving her another kiss. "I might not be able to buy you diamonds every day, but I think I can give you a few things that could be more . . . satisfying."

From the lustful grin on his face, she could imagine all the ways he was thinking of satisfying her.

"You think we can work on that tonight after dinner at my place?"

# Melting the Snow

# Chapter Eight

CiCi and Daniel came up with the best story they could think of in the small amount of time they had. When Samantha couldn't hold back his work commitments any longer, CiCi gave Daniel one last kiss and set off for home.

Daniel's meeting with Phillip went as planned. It was when their business was done that Daniel began to sweat.

"Now all of that is out of the way, I have to admit I'm curious about you and CiCi. It's none of my business, of course, but . . ."

Daniel knew Phillip well enough to realize he was fishing for information.

"You want to know why we've kept all of it a secret?"

"If you don't mind telling me."

"We met about six months ago and began dating. After the whole fiasco with Lena, we went away for a while. I proposed while we were on the trip, but it was CiCi's idea to go ahead and get married. We haven't told our families and haven't even officially moved in together yet. The plan was to tell everyone over the holidays and have a little renewal and reception. I told CiCi I wanted her lawyers to draft a Post-Nuptial agreement before we announced anything to the press for fear of gold digger rumors."

Phillip shook his head. "I can understand. The last man she publically dated was a real ass. I couldn't believe he stole her mother's jewelry."

Daniel's chest ached at the thought of someone hurting CiCi in such a horrible manor.

"I want to protect her. We weren't planning on telling anyone, but I wore my ring the first day by accident. When it seemed to keep all the females at bay, I kept wearing it." The moment had come to beg Phillip for his silence, but something unexpected happened.

"Don't worry about me saying anything about it."

Daniel smiled and released a sigh of relief. "Thank you. You don't understand how much I appreciate it. Simone kind of took us by surprise when we bumped into her at the coffee shop this morning. We hadn't thought about what would happen if we saw someone from work while we were out together."

Phillip picked up his phone and dialed. "Simone, could you come to my office now, please?"

Daniel heard a soft response, and Simone was knocking on the door within a minute.

"Yes, come in and close the door behind you."

Simone came and sat in the chair next to Daniel, her usual smile screwed in place.

"What can I help you with?"

Phillip looked to Daniel to begin.

"Well, I wanted to ask you if you would mind keeping my relationship with CiCi to yourself. It was such of a spur of the moment decision, and we haven't got everything in place to announce it yet."

Simone let her mask slip a bit when her cheeks paled. "I'm sorry, Daniel, but I think it's too late."

"Too late?" His pulse skyrocketed at the implication that she had run her mouth already.

"Yes." She pulled out her phone and brought up a local news website. "It appears someone took some photos of the two of you Friday night and this morning."

Daniel took the phone away from her and began to read the article.

*It looks like New York's most eligible bachelorette is off the market. Heiress to the Newport billions, illustrator and author CiCi Newport was seen with a man we've identified as Daniel Digby. Digby, 28, is a senior consultant for Henderson Public Relations. An inside source says Digby and Newport spent most of Friday evening in Marco St. Croix's VIP section at his newest club, Chameleon.*

Daniel studied the picture of the two of them talking at their table and one of them kissing on the dance floor. His stomach began to churn, and he wasn't through reading yet.

*If the rumors are true, it looks like Miss Newport is actually Mrs. Digby now. Our source tells us Digby has recently married, but his bride's identity is a mystery. From the look of these pictures of the couple in a coffee shop this morning, we are confident in reporting Newport and Digby are more than friends.*

*To keep up to date on this story, please sign up for our email alerts. When we know it, you'll know it.*

Daniel looked over to see a tiny smile on Simone's face. He handed Simone her phone while all the pieces began to fit into place. "You took these pictures?"

"What? No, of course not," she answered with a sideways glance to Phillip. "That is absurd, Phillip."

"I feel sick." Daniel placed his head between his knees. Maybe she didn't want him after all. He had a feeling she wanted much more: his job.

Phillip picked up his phone and made another call, but Daniel couldn't hear what he was saying. His world was crashing around him. Simone had made CiCi tabloid fodder over a job. It could have been much worse but the fact was the lie was out there and he had no idea how to fix everything.

"Daniel, come on." Samantha pulled on his shoulders so he was sitting upright. "Let me get you to your office, and we can call CiCi."

"I'm so sorry, Phillip," Daniel said in a daze.

"No worries, Daniel. You talk to CiCi and let me know what you want your next step to be. We would be happy to send out a press release on your behalf when you're ready."

"Yes, thank you. I will let you know."

Samantha led Daniel into his office and locked the door behind them. "I've already had several calls asking for confirmation. I have responded with 'no comment' thus far."

"Right." Daniel shook his head. *Get it together. Focus on CiCi.* "I need to call CiCi." He dug his phone out of his pocket and dialed. Samantha motioned that she was leaving, but he shook his head and gestured for her to sit.

"Hello," CiCi answered with a sniffle.

"Oh, God. You've heard already, haven't you?"

"Yes," she stated softly.

"I am so sorry. I can't believe how fast this has gotten out of hand."

"It's not your fault. They had the pictures from Friday night. Even if we hadn't bumped into Simone this morning, I am sure they would have come out. I'm not upset about that. It's Reggie."

"Reggie?" He had to think for a moment. Yes, she had told him Reggie was like a father to her. "He knows?"

"Yes, and he didn't take it well. His blood pressure shot up, and he passed out."

"Christ! Is he okay?"

"Yes. He's resting now, but he wants to talk with both of us. I didn't have time to explain what was going on."

"I'm sorry I have caused such a mess." Daniel felt his eyes well up and turned his chair so Samantha wouldn't see his tears fall.

"It was a shock, of course, but I think it will be a good thing. I talked with Lori already, and she has been fielding calls all day about my book launch. I got a call from one of Oprah's producers who I've been friends with for years, offering congratulations and asking to do an interview with Oprah herself."

"Wow." Daniel was gobsmacked. He'd thought his white lie would ruin her life, but it seemed as though it might not be so bad after all. "What's our next move? I'll do whatever you want."

"I think it would be best if you come over and stay with me for a while. The press is already camped out front. I can send a car with security to pick you up. We can talk over dinner."

Daniel nodded to himself. "Yes, that's a good idea. Can you arrange it for an hour from now?"

"Not a problem. I will have the driver give

you a call when he is on his way."

"All right."

The line was silent for several long seconds before CiCi spoke. "It will be okay, Daniel."

"Yeah?"

"Yes. I think maybe this is what both of us have been looking for." Her voice sounded hopeful, a feeling he was beginning to share.

"I think you might be right. I'll see you soon." They ended the call, and he turned his chair around to see Samantha had left his office.

He took a minute to collect his thoughts but was interrupted by Samantha's voice on his intercom. "Daniel, your mother is on line two."

# Melting the Snow

# Chapter Nine

"Don't you worry about Reggie. He's fine." Marcy continued to chop the vegetables for their salad.

"I hope so. Daniel feels awful about the whole thing." CiCi looked at the clock for the eighth time in the last ten minutes. "He should be here soon."

"Now that I know what is *really* going on, what are you going to do?"

That was the billion-dollar question. She knew what she wanted. It was so clear and vibrant, she could almost see it. Convincing Daniel would be the first problem. After that, convincing the rest of the world could be more challenging than anything she had ever done in her life.

"I have an idea, but I need to talk to Daniel and Randolph."

Marcy stopped mid chop. "Randolph?" She put her knife down and walked over to stand in front of CiCi. "Are you sure?"

"If Daniel agrees, yes, I'm sure." Randolph had been Winston Newport's best friend and the family attorney for decades. While CiCi had lawyers and accountants handling her assets from her father's estate, Randolph handled the personal issues. He read their father's will to CiCi and Bridgett the day after his death. She'd drawn up her own will with him a few weeks later at the tender age of sixteen. This time, he would need to draft a prenuptial agreement.

Marcy put her hands on CiCi's shoulders and looked her in the eye. "You really want to marry him?"

"I know you think I'm crazy."

"Oh, baby girl." Marcy cupped her cheek with one hand. "Not crazy. Maybe a bit rash, but not crazy. You've only known him for a few weeks. You were with Jensen for two years, and you know what a rat bastard he turned out to be."

CiCi nodded at the memory of the man with whom she'd thought she would share her life. "Daniel is not Jensen. I think he's the cure to the curse that has held my life for so long."

Marcy leaned in and gave her a kiss on the cheek before wrapping her in a motherly hug. "I want you safe and happy. If he can do both, I approve."

"Thank you," CiCi whispered while she clung to the woman she thought of as a second mother.

"CiCi?" Daniel called from the entryway.

CiCi took Marcy's hand and led her out of the kitchen.

He stood in the entryway taking off his coat and gloves next to the burly security guard who waited at the door.

"Thanks for getting him here safe, Rick."

"Not a problem, Miss Newport. The press is getting a bit out of hand. I have called in some more men and informed NYPD. I will let you know if any problems arise."

"I appreciate it, Rick."

He nodded and went out through the front door.

Daniel wrapped his arms around CiCi and gave her a chaste kiss. "I'm so happy to have you in my arms again."

"I'm happy to be here." She glided her hands over his chest and around his neck to give him a kiss that showed him indeed how happy she was.

"Oh, hell."

CiCi froze at the sound of Reggie's voice coming from the stairs. She pulled back and took Daniel's hand tight in hers, ready to make the introductions.

"Daniel, I'd like you to meet Reggie and Marcy Raeburn. They run the house and are my second parents."

"It's a pleasure to meet you, Mr. and Mrs. Raeburn." He held out his hand to Reggie.

Reggie stared at it for a moment before he made a grunting sound and turned to go into the kitchen.

"Forgive my husband, Daniel. He hasn't been filled in yet." Marcy shook Daniel's outstretched hand.

"I suppose we should clear things up." He took both of CiCi's hands in his own. "Lead the way to wherever that delicious smell is coming from."

They found Reggie in the kitchen taking a few of his pills, followed by a swig of water.

"Reggie, we can explain." CiCi left Daniel's side to go to the older man. "Let's sit and eat, and we will tell you what is really going on."

~*~*~

"I see." Reggie took a sip from his glass of water. "That makes me want to kill you a little bit less."

Daniel paled at the older man's glare after they'd explained his relationship with CiCi and the events of earlier in the day.

"He's kidding." Marcy assured him. "I can see how happy you've made our girl over the past couple of weeks. That makes you okay in my book."

"Thank you, Mrs. Raeburn." Daniel calmed a bit. He looked across the table to see a beautiful smile gracing CiCi's lips.

"Now, you've both made this mess . . ." Reggie pointed his knife at Daniel, and then at CiCi. "What are you going to do about it?"

"It's something Daniel and I need to discuss. Alone." CiCi glared at Reggie, and Daniel noticed Reggie scowling right back, as if they were having their own silent argument. At last, CiCi conceded. "Fine. I think we should get married. Happy now?"

Daniel's fork clattered against his plate when it fell from his fingers. He felt three pairs of eyes on him while he stared at his almost clean plate. The idea began to sink in, the edges of a dream creeping forward in his mind.

"Married?" he whispered. He looked and caught the worried look on CiCi's face.

There was no terror or distinct nausea like there had been when Missy broached the subject years ago. A warm of wave contentment filled him from head to toe. The moment his life would change forever had arrived.

"I would be honored to be your husband."

CiCi raised a brow. "But?"

"No but." Daniel got up from his seat and walked around the table to stand beside CiCi's chair. He turned it a little to make enough room for him to get down on one knee in front of her. He took a deep breath and offered his hand. She slipped hers into it without hesitation. "Since the first moment I saw you, you've been a constant in my mind. I feel privileged I got to know you as the girl from the coffee shop and not the 'billionaire beauty'." He quoted the nickname used in one of the articles that had hit the Internet earlier in the day. "We have both tried to plan our lives without too much success. I can live my life without a plan as long as you are there beside me. Will you marry me?"

"Yes." CiCi took his hand from hers and placed it on her cheek.

Daniel got down on both knees and brought her face to his. She wrapped her arms around his neck, and he gave into the feeling of complete fulfillment.

"When?" he asked once he pulled away.

"Um . . ." She tipped her head to stare at the ceiling, tears running from her eyes. "I hadn't thought that far."

He stood and pulled her into his arms. "What about Christmas Eve here? Can you get your family here by then?"

"Yes, I think so. I want it small, just family and a few friends."

Marcy clapped her hands. "We can do it here at the house. We can put the tree in the living room and arrange the room so you can say your vows in front of it. This will be perfect. Oh!" She grabbed Reggie's hand. "We have to start decorating right away."

"We're getting married," CiCi whispered in awe while Daniel held her tight in his arms.

"Maybe we should start practicing on the Honeymoon."

~*~*~

CiCi hummed her favorite Christmas carols while she worked through her morning routine. Freshly showered and smelling of her favorite body wash, she entered her bedroom to the most beautiful sight she had ever seen in her bed: a half-naked fiancé.

"Morning," she whispered in his ear before giving him a kiss on the cheek.

"Mmmmmmmm." Daniel stretched his arms above his head before wrapping them around her. "I swear that was the best night's sleep I've ever had."

"This bed is top of the line, and these sheets are the softest I could find."

"Yes." He kissed the top of her head. "An added bonus, but I think the company and the activities in this bed were the best parts."

"Is that so, Mr. Digby?"

"Yes, it is." He placed a kiss on her forehead. "What do we need to do today? Phillip has given me the day off, so I'm at your disposal."

"I'm sure Marcy has most of the wedding planned already. I need to call Bridgett and Emily. You'll need to talk to your family, too, right?"

"I talked to my mom yesterday."

CiCi sat up and looked at him. "What did you say?"

"She was so excited, I couldn't tell her the truth. I told her you are beautiful and brilliant woman, and she was lucky to have you as a daughter-in-law. She wants to meet you as soon as possible. I don't think I will be able to hold her off for long."

The thought of another mother figure in

her life excited CiCi. If his mother was anything like Daniel, CiCi was sure to love her.

"One problem, though." Daniel sat against the headboard. "I have none of my clothes or things here. Do you think I could get my friend, Gabe, to pick up some things and bring them over?"

"Sure. I can have Rick meet him downstairs and make sure he gets in all right."

"Okay, I'll call Gabe, and you can call Bridgett. Then it's off to face Marcy. Should I be scared?"

"Very."

# *Chapter Ten*

The press release came out the next day, stating CiCi and Daniel recently had a private ceremony and would be celebrating their marriage with their family and close friends over the holidays. It didn't satisfy the press much, but Daniel was able to return to work after a few days.

Over the course of the week, Daniel moved his things over to CiCi's house. He was lucky enough to be able to keep the couch the he loved since CiCi had space for it on the top floor. Even his small Christmas tree found a spot in his new home, a small table in the corner of *their* bedroom.

With each small piece of himself revealed, CiCi shared a piece of herself. She took him into her most sacred space: her studio. Reggie and Marcy rarely ever got a peek in there, but she let Daniel in. He watched in rapt fascination while she worked for hours on her latest project.

Their physical relationship had developed, as well. Her studio, the shower, and the chilly rooftop garden all had exciting new memories of the intimacy they'd shared. They had both fallen fast and hard, but they were still holding back on making their final declarations. After hours upon hours of thought, Daniel decided he would have to be the one to speak first.

The day of CiCi's book launch had arrived. She was stunned to see so many people waiting to get her book in The Strand Book Store. The areas of the store that weren't packed with books were filled with people. Parents with eager children huddled in the space where she would be doing her talk and signing.

Daniel gave her a short pep talk and quick kiss before sending her out to face the masses.

She was stunned by the thunderous applause when she walked out to address the crowd.

"Good morning! Thank you all so much for coming today." CiCi picked up a copy of *Santa's Shoulder* and held it in front her. "This book was inspired by a conversation I had with Santa about two years ago. I was having a bad day, like so many of us do, and Santa was there to make it all better. It got me thinking about all the things Santa has to deal with and how many people come to him with their problems. This is the story of how Santa deals with everything the world puts on his shoulders." She sat, opened the book, and began reading to a captive audience.

After she was finished signing, the store was filled with the sound of jingling bells, followed by a robust "Ho, ho, ho!"

The same black boots with silver buckles,

red velvet trousers, matching coat with fur trim, long, real hair and beard, rosy cheeks, and twinkling blue eyes from her illustrations appeared. A tear rolled down her cheek when she realized it was the same Santa from the party almost two years earlier, the living embodiment of her inspiration.

He waved to a group of excited children before he approached CiCi. "Merry Christmas, CiCi." He took both of her hands in his.

"Merry Christmas, Santa. I didn't know you would be here."

"It was a spur of the moment decision. Mrs. Claus took charge for the day so I could be here. I am proud of you, CiCi. Thank you for telling this story."

She shook her head since she was choked up and unable to say anything further.

Daniel walked behind her and placed a hand on her shoulder. "Everything okay?"

"Wonderful," she said, sniffing and wiping away another tear.

"Thank you for coming, Santa. I see you got my letter."

"I'm happy to be here, Daniel." He squeezed CiCi's hands. "I see something wondrous has happened."

"Yes, it has. We couldn't be happier." CiCi looked at Daniel to see a brilliant smile that matched her own.

"Oh, I don't know. I might have something

to make you a bit happier." Santa pulled a small box out of his coat pocket. "Open it."

She took the small box and found a black velvet box nestled inside. Her breath caught in her throat when she lifted the lid.

"Daniel wrote me a letter telling me how much he wanted to find your mother's wedding ring to give to you. With a little magic and luck, we were able to locate it."

The silver band with diamonds embedded in it was a sight CiCi had never thought she would see again. She picked it out of the box and noticed the engraving inside the band. "All my love," she whispered.

"I believe Daniel has something to tell you." Santa turned CiCi around to face Daniel.

Daniel took the ring from between her fingertips and took her left hand. "I knew that if there were any ring that would be good enough to rest on your finger, it would be this one. This ring symbolizes the great love experienced by your parents and the love I hope to share with you for the rest of my life. I know everything has happened so fast, but I wouldn't have had it any other way. I love you and will spend every day showing you how much." He slipped the ring on her finger.

"But how?" CiCi kept her eyes focused on the ring, afraid that if she looked away it might disappear.

"Like Santa said, magic and luck."

"Thank you." She wrapped her arms around his neck and hugged him tight. "I love that you arranged all this, finding the ring and inviting Santa. I love you, Daniel."

Daniel let out a sigh of relief and held her as tight as she was holding him. He looked over her shoulder and caught Santa winking at him. He winked back.

As much as Daniel had enjoyed Christmas over the years, he knew without a doubt, this would be the best Christmas ever.

# Melting the Snow

# Epilogue

"You bitch," Emily grumbled.

"Emily!" Bridgett reprimanded.

"Mom, she looks amazing. Admit it; neither of us looked that good on our wedding days."

CiCi laughed while her sister and niece argued about how beautiful she looked. She turned to ask her almost sister-in-law, Daisy, a question and noticed her crying.

"Daisy?" CiCi walked over to Daisy and took her by the elbow. "What's wrong?"

"It's just," she sniffled. "I don't have this with my other sisters-in-law. We've never had any good times like these, especially before their weddings." CiCi handed her a tissue. "Thanks. You know Jeff's wife, Willow?" CiCi nodded. "She screamed at all her bridesmaids, including me, about how horrid we all looked up until we walked down the aisle. Hank's wife, Katie, passed out before the ceremony started, and he pretty much held her upright during the entire service. Bruce's wife, Rhonda, was drunk the entire day. I was not looking forward to today after living through three of my other brother's weddings."

"Oh, honey." CiCi brought Daisy into her arms. "I'm so sorry you had to go through that, but I'm not like them." She pulled away and wiped a tear from Daisy's cheek. "You are Daniel's twin sister. From what I've heard from him and what I've learned spending time with you, we are going to be great friends."

"That means so much to me. At least it won't be three against one anymore." Daisy giggled.

"I've got your back, sister." CiCi smiled at the happiness reflected in Daisy's eyes.

"Let's give you one last look before we head down, okay?" Bridgett led CiCi over to the mirror to give her final approval before they went downstairs to where Daniel and their wedding guests were waiting.

Her dress was simple, yet elegant. It was the only one she'd tried on. She had known the strapless ivory gown was *the* dress the moment she laid eyes on it. It didn't have a train or pounds of lace. It was unpretentious and beautiful, like she had always dreamed.

She didn't wear a veil, only a diamond-studded hair comb that had belonged to her father's mother. Her makeup was light, and her natural beauty shined through.

"I think I'm ready." CiCi took a couple of deep breaths to steady her nerves.

"Let's get on with this. I can't take the smells of everything Marcy has in the kitchen much longer." Emily opened the door and motioned for the ladies to get moving.

"Please, don't talk about food," CiCi groaned. "I haven't had the stomach to eat all day."

"Nerves or morning sickness?" Emily joked.

CiCi whacked her on the shoulder. "Nerves. This is not a shotgun wedding." She glared at Emily so that she'd keep her mouth closed.

"Ladies," Bridgett admonished. "I can hear Daniel pacing down there. Can we go before the poor man wears a hole in the carpet?"

~*~*~

The second CiCi stepped into his view on Bridgett's arm, Daniel knew every twist and turn in his life had been worth it to be with her now. Her eyes met his, and they didn't leave until Bridgett kissed her cheek and placed her hand in Daniel's in front of their twelve foot tall Christmas tree.

The judge said a few words, the bride and groom responding at the right moments. They exchanged vows and rings with a few tears, and then kissed to seal their union.

The small group of family and friends congratulated them with toast after toast during the dinner Marcy had prepared. CiCi couldn't imagine a more perfect day.

"You know, we've set ourselves up by doing this on Christmas Eve," Daniel said during their first dance as husband and wife.

"How so?"

"No other holiday will ever top this."

CiCi leaned in and kissed her new husband. "You don't think ringing in the New Year in our private Hawaiian villa can top this?"

"I don't know how. Today has been perfect." He sighed and ran her fingers through the brunette waves cascading down her back.

"Today we are surrounded by friends and family."

"And?"

"In Hawaii," she whispered in his ear. "We will be alone and naked the entire time." CiCi kissed along his jaw and felt him shiver.

"You're right; that might take the top spot. On the other hand, if we kick everyone out now, lock ourselves in our room, and not surface until the twenty-sixth, maybe . . ." Daniel pulled her in closer, nuzzling at her neck.

"We'll call it a tie. Let's get to kicking."

## The End

# *Author Biography*

Lindsey Gray dreamed of several different careers as a child. On the short list were doctor, chef, and actress. None held her attention as much as putting pen to paper and creating her own world through words. Since 2010, she has published three novels and one short story with The Writer's Coffee Shop Publishing House. In 2013, she went on her first self-publishing adventure and produced her novella, "Fireworks."
A mid-west native, Lindsey enjoys spending time with her husband and two children, rooting for the Green Bay Packers, reading whatever she can get her hands on, and making life interesting at every turn.

**Her works include:**
*Lies Inside*
*Redemption* (The Redemption Series, Book 1)
*Revisited* (The Redemption Series, Book 2)
*Fireworks*
*Not the Same Season*

# Melting the Snow

# *Frozen Moments*

By

## Michele Richard

# Melting the Snow

# *Acknowledgements*

First, let me say "thank you" to the
Renaissance Romance Publishing editing
staff. No author is ever perfect the first time
they draft a new novel.
Without my family none of this would have
been possible. They have given me all the
support I could have asked for. I love you,
Virginia and Danielle.
This book is dedicated to my mom, Patricia.
She was my rock until she lost her battle
with cancer. I will always love her. The
lessons she taught me will guide me for the
rest of my life.

# Melting the Snow

# Contents

# Melting the Snow

# Chapter One

## *2012*

# *Everything Has a Beginning*

Melanie Shepherd's high-heel boots clicked off the concrete as she approached Blackie's Boxing on 7th Street in South Boston. It had been years since she'd been there last. Of course, back then it had been nothing more than a pile of rubble. Not that now there was much more to look at — at least the walls were still standing. So many things would soon be changing. The best she could hope for was a better outcome. She'd known this moment was coming, even been waiting for it. That only seemed to heighten the anxiety building within her. In order to achieve her goal, she'd been approved to relinquish certain information — information that was generally reserved.

The Sentinel Order guarded how much information was allotted to possible new recruits. This case was no different. Well, maybe it was. Elysian would be one of humanity's greatest warriors for correcting the future if he chose to join the cause.

A stress-filled laugh trickled from Melanie's mauve painted lips when she reached out and grasped the tarnished brass doorknob. At thirty, she felt like a sixteen-year-old going to a party where the boy she had a crush on lay in wait — not that she actually ever experienced that feeling. The upcoming conversation would seem like something from the Twilight Zone to Elysian; for Melanie, it was an all too real past.

Even with the harsh October wind, common to New England's fall, whipping her long auburn hair, the heated air blasted Melanie in the face when she yanked open the red-painted wooden door. Sparse sounds of leather impacting skin and grunts of exertion drifted her way. She'd chosen this time because she knew the gym would be nearly empty and that served her purpose perfectly.

Melanie's focus drifted toward the single punching bag to the left. There stood the main reason for the five a.m. visit. She took a moment to appreciate the view. At nearly six feet tall, he was long and lean and built for boxing. His broad shoulders and taut muscles showed his years of training. Red and white satin boxing shorts hung low on his hips, revealing his defined abdominal muscles. So lost in her appreciation of his body, she hadn't realized he had noticed her standing there.

"Can I help you?" Elysian mumbled around his mouth piece, holding his gloved hands up in question.

Putting an added confidence in her stride, Melanie approached the target. "My name is Melanie Shepherd. And you are Elysian Del Rey, or Ely to your friends. You're named after Greek mythology, the Elysian Fields in Elysium. Said to be the final resting place of the souls of the heroic and the virtuous."

Shocked by her declaration, he furrowed his brow in apparent confusion. So much about him was different, yet still the same. His short, spiked, blond hair beckoned her fingers to run through it. Of course, now it had a lot less gray. She smiled, thinking about how his blue eyes were no longer lined with the wrinkles that once marked his age.

Stepping back, Ely popped the plastic guard from his mouth to his hand. "How did you know that?"

Melanie laughed, knowing how ridiculous her next statement would sound. "You will tell me about fifteen years from now."

"No one outside my family knows that. Why would I tell you? I don't even know you," Ely huffed, turning and stomping toward the bench where his black workout bag sat.

"You will." She shook her head, her shoulder-length, auburn hair swayed with her movements. "Just not here or now."

"That makes no sense, lady," he growled, using his teeth to pull away the Velcro strap to one of his boxing gloves.

"Let me buy you a coffee and I'll explain everything."

Shaking his head, Ely smiled for the first time since Melanie had walked in. "Is this how you get all your dates?"

"Nope, you're the first."

"This had better be good, and don't expect me to shower first."

"Wouldn't dream of it."

Tossing his gear back in his bag, Ely headed back to the changing room. He had no idea what to make of Melanie Shepherd and her strange ramblings; though he couldn't fight the fact she was easy on the eyes. Her reddish hair and gray eyes drew him in and held him there. There was also something about the way she held herself. An aura of confidence surrounded her. She was strong without being full of herself.

~*~*~

Five minutes after Ely left Melanie in the sparring area, he returned dressed in his usual black T-shirt and worn denim jeans. It just so happened, he had the day off from the gas station where he worked as an auto mechanic. In exchange for working Saturdays, he alternated one day a week off depending on which day was slow. Rafe never harassed Ely about taking time off. He knew he'd get his forty hours.

Melanie stood leaning against the white-painted concrete wall near the door with her arms crossed her over her chest, watching Salvador working out on the heavy bag. From the way she watched him, she knew what to look for, maybe she represented boxers? It still didn't explain how she knew about Ely.

Walking up, he nodded to the door. "You ready to go?"

"It's the whole reason I'm here." She laughed, waving to proceed with her hand.

Ely couldn't help feeling this would be a long day if she kept up with cryptic hints. He held the door open, allowing her to pass through it first, noticing how she checked her watch. More so, he noticed the watch. It wasn't anything like he'd ever seen before. The solid-metal cuff-band resembled what was his best guess: titanium, but it didn't sound right. No one made watches like that that he knew of. The crystal face glowed a luminescent yellow with black digits, but they didn't look like any numbers he knew.

Trying not to obviously stare at her jewelry, he followed her out the door and down the street to the local Starbucks. Though he was a Dunkin Donut's man, if she was buying, he'd deal with it.

"Grab a seat in the corner while I grab our coffees," Melanie instructed.

"Sure—I'll have . . ." Her laughter stopped his order.

"Yeah, I know: black, no sugar."

Shaking his head, Ely dropped his bag and slipped off his black leather coat, swinging it over the back of the chair, opting to keep on his black hoodie. Melanie Shepherd was good if she knew how he took his coffee.

Ely slipped into the seat and started strumming his fingertips on the white Formica tabletop. Melanie was an enigma to him. She knew too much about him for someone he didn't know. Had she researched him? Had someone following him?

"I can see the gears in your mind working." Melanie's voice dragged him back from his inner ramblings.

Ely heaved a heavy breath as Melanie sat in the chair across from him. "Just trying to figure out your gig. You talk and act like you know me when this is first time I've ever seen you."

"What I'm about to tell you is going to sound a little far-fetched and pretty unbelievable. You've been chosen to join a select team of individuals on a voluntary series of missions."

Leaning back in his seat, he crossed his arms and pursed his lips. "Like for the government?"

Melanie cradled the cup in her hands and leaned closer, allowing her whisper to be heard only by Ely. "For humanity."

There was no explaining why his anger raged; it just did. He slammed his fists on the table and jumped up. "Again with the coded word crap."

Melanie laughed, unaffected by his outburst. "Sit back down, Ely. The Sentinels have already approved me giving you further information."

"And who the hell are they?" he snipped, sitting back down.

"The Sentinel Order live in your future. They are the Keepers of Time. Each Sentinel stands as guardians for those who were once the gifted and proclaimed golden-children of the greatest government's scientific communities. In the not-so-far-off future, life as you know it will cease to exist."

It took everything in him not to burst out laughing. Either this lady fell off her meds or someone had set him up for one of those ridiculous reality shows. Regardless, he wasn't biting, but that didn't mean he couldn't play along long enough to get the hell out of Dodge.

"How could you possibly know that?" Popping off the lid entirely, he lifted his cup, taking his first sip.

Melanie's smile widened before she answered, "Because I'm not from your time; I'm from theirs."

Ely sputtered, all but spitting his blistering, hot coffee in her face. "Excuse me?"

"The answer to both questions is no, Ely. I have not fallen off my meds and no one has set you up for a reality show."

"How did you know what I was thinking?"

Smiling into her cup, Melanie took a sip. "You told me about it. It was one of my favorite bedtime stories."

"Bedtime stories?"

"I told you, I'm from their time, even though I was technically born in 2006." As proof, she slid her birth certificate across the table, not that Ely could have spotted a forgery from an original when he looked at it. "You found me in the winter of 2021, just outside Cambridge, when I was sixteen. The Nexus, The Sentinels, and our Matrix are located at MIT. You are the reason I work for The Sentinel Order."

"So, I'm supposed to believe you're a time traveler? And I suppose you have a lot of time traveling friends walking around, right?" Ely smirked, a laugh falling from his lips.

"I guess you could say I am. And no, I'm alone. The compounds needed to send me back were depleted with my teleportation. Resources in the future are hard to come by. We had to scrounge for every little required element." Melanie's gray eyes burned with emotions Ely couldn't deny. "With the collapse of the world as you knew it, the scientific world now hides and tries to correct the downfalls that led to the end of your way of life. Don't take their sacrifices lightly. They gave up everything: friends, families, and loved ones to fix this mess. I should know."

"You have to understand my side. I'm just supposed to sit here and believe what you're telling me? I'm sorry, sweetie. The world doesn't work that way."

"I never expected you to believe me. The invitation for coffee was always to show you." Melanie looked at her watch then held up her fingers, counting off the seconds. "One – Two – Three." With a grin gracing her lips, she nodded her head, indicating to look around the room.

Ely's breath hitched in his throat as his eyes darted from customer to customer. The document slipped from his fingers and landed on the table. No one was moving. Each patron looked like a mannequin in a store window. Even the coffee the staff was pouring stopped its motion. The only sound in the room came from Melanie and Ely's breathing.

"Why is everything frozen?"

"They did it from my time. Very few are immune to our ability to freeze time. That's why I'm here: for you. We want you to work with our team in your present timeline."

Ely suddenly found himself struggling to keep up with what he was seeing and what she was saying; she wasn't nut job like he thought. He looked out the window to see even the people on the sidewalk were frozen.

"What exactly do you do?"

"We have a team of technically-altered volunteers who save those they can and correct the flawed outcomes that threaten to create the catastrophic future. They're faster, stronger, and more agile than those living in your timeline. They report to me. I get my orders from the Sentinels."

"If the Sentinels are in the future, how do you get your orders from them?"

"I have a lab at MIT. We've created a Nexus, or bridging, if you will. In layman's terms, it's a tear in time where our computers are connected. It consumes a lot of power. The head of my department is a future Sentinel, and privy to the knowledge of what I do to some extent. He doesn't know all the details, but he does know enough to assist me. I won't go into the technical details right now. Should you decide to join the team, I can promise you a tour and further explanation of how it all works. Get ready. One – Two – Three." Eli shook his head when his ears popped. His head spun as the sounds came rushing back and the motions of everyone and everything around him began to swirl. "Little dizzying, isn't it? You get used to it. The first time is always the hardest."

"Um — yeah. This is a lot to take in. It's not something I can decide on the spot. I do have a few more questions before I can decide. You said that the team was technically-altered, how so?"

"Your scientists would call it a form of nanotechnology for short; in 2015 they perfected it. Nanobotic implants give our team the upper hand. By no means are they superheroes. They're not infallible, they do die. What does that mean? They enhance your general genetics. Those muscles you've spent years perfecting will be even stronger, those five-minute miles even shorter, and should you receive a non-life threatening injury, the bots will repair the damage quicker."

"How long until I have to decide?"

"I'll walk you to your car." Without another word, Melanie stood.

Ely took her hint. The conversation was over until they were out of public ear. Standing up, he grabbed his bag and coat before following her to the door. From the way they marched out the door and across the street, you could barely tell they were together. He had to stifle a laugh when she knew exactly where he parked his car behind the gym. Melanie didn't say a word until she stopped at his blue Subaru sedan. She spun on her heel, already holding two vibrantly glowing tubes.

"The red vial will shut off the neural pathways that prevent you from freezing. The green one will change your DNA to prepare you for the journey ahead of you. Choice is yours." Melanie's hands shook slightly when she placed the tubes in Ely's.

"A little Alice in Wonderland, isn't it?" Ely couldn't help but feel he'd been shoved down the rabbit hole as the fairy tale went.

"Just a bit. You have twenty-four hours to decide before the compounds become inert and the nanobotics shut down. Once they cease to illuminate, the choice is made for you."

Grasping the two vials in his fist, he wasn't sure twenty-four hours was enough time. "How will I contact you with my answer?"

"You won't need to." Her reply came as just a whisper as she turned and walked away.

# Chapter Two

## 2045

# Life as a Not So Happily Ever After

Ely sprinted down the side corridor headed toward the Nexus. He'd been eating lunch when the warning lights and sirens went off in the guarded underground section of the Nexus. In their future, a single group of surviving scientists had forged a Nexus of information, past images, and wealth of knowledge in a broadband of specialties, most of those centering on technology and physics.

The Sentinel Order had a scheduled meeting to discuss the next mission on the list of potential changes to the timeline later in the week. Something more urgent must have come in. It had been years since Ely had partaken in the actual time change. Those days were long over. Now, in his sixties, his days were filled on the other end of missions. Even though the missions they'd completed hadn't corrected the collapse, they had to be completed again in a re-looping effect with new missions added in. Somewhere in the mix, something had to work; they just had to find the right combination.

"Ely!"

Looking over his shoulder, he saw another Sentinel exiting his quarters. "Salvador, any word from Melanie?"

He and Salvador Torres had been friends since before the early inception of the Order. They'd boxed at the same gym when the world went to pieces. Together, the pair had helped formed the group. In the early years, it was to save the scientists who couldn't protect themselves from the savages preying on the weak. Wild packs of nomads moved from one area to another, stripping the cities of food and resources. Killing became part of the normal process. One less person to feed.

"No. Apparently the younger you is just as stubborn as the older you." He laughed, jogging up and slapping Ely on the back.

Ely shook his head. "I had hoped my advice would have made it easier."

The pair darted around the final corner that would lead them to the continuum capsule. "Not likely. Melanie will have her hands full with you at any age. I just hope all her careful planning wasn't wasted."

"I just pray she finds what she was searching for. She always deserved better than this world." Salvador waited for Ely to enter the Nexus core first.

Melanie had been sixteen and orphaned when he found her scavenging a collapsed building for food in Somerville. The frail teen was on the edge of starvation. Her platinum eyes widened with fear when she saw him approaching her. To a young woman, the thirty-year-old man lurking in the dark must have looked intimidating. In those days, they'd just begun getting power back on in larger areas.

Then again, back then, all men were intimidating. Savagery had taken hold of the world and men. Women of any age had genuine fears, but not from Ely, he could never hurt them or take from their bodies what they didn't give willingly.

Of course, Ely knew immediately who Melanie Shepherd was and who she would become, having already met her in this past. It was odd. In his younger days, she was the one who knew him first from when he was older; in her younger days, it was he who knew her first. One couldn't happen without the other. Their lives were forever looped together in an endless time circle.

With every time course change, fear gripped Ely's heart. Would this be the one?

It had taken hours and several cans of fruit cocktail to get Melanie to tell Ely her name. Once she opened up, she'd latched on and there was no turning back. With her tiny hand in his, they headed toward the safety and security his home provided. From that day on, he'd been the one to raise her after he'd brought her into the inner sanctum of the Matrix.

The Matrix was their hidden world below ground. A series of tunnels and collapsed infrastructures connected to make up a new world safe from those looking to destroy the remains of civility.

In the beginning, people fought to help each other, saving not only friends and family, but perfect strangers hurt in the streets. Then the reality sunk in and hope was lost. People started to realize that help wasn't coming. The darkest days after the shock wore off could never be erased from the survivor's minds. Those horrific memories were forever.

Slowly over the years, the members of the Order took back the upper floors, then the streets, and finally the entire MIT campus after the entire area had been barricaded in by ten foot makeshift walls and renamed Salvation. Other settlements of populations popped up in other parts of the city and those cities and towns in the general area during the same time. Some were friendly, some were to be avoided. They'd managed to make alliances, open up trade lines, and spread their borders.

One thing all the settlements had in common: the desire to make the future better. Any communities with a scientist were asked to have them relocated to the Matrix.

The keyword had been asked. Once they saw what was offered in the research departments, most readily agreed, and those who didn't were returned to their homes.

"Any new reports?" Jeremiah drew Ely's attention back from his recollection.

He looked up, shaking his head. "Nothing new from my side. If I'd joined the team, I should be feeling the effects by now as you all had."

Each Sentinel had been approached first in their earlier years to join the correction team. If anyone was going to know the secrets of what they did, they needed to know they could trust them. To date, Salvador, Foster, and Jeremiah had joined Melanie's team in the other timeline.

Looking around the room, they each wore the scars from the effects already. Yesterday, Salvador developed a scar just under his hairline that, luckily, his brown, shaggy mop would cover. Last week, one revealed itself below Foster's left, black eyebrow, barely missing his hazel eye. Jeremiah's was less dramatic and more of a nip to his lower lip.

Ely called the room to attention. "Let's hear it."

"We have a new target," Foster called as he tapped away at his console station.

"Share it on the overhead," Ely ordered. The crystal flat-screen pane of glass illuminated with an old, faded video footage.

"What are we looking for?"

"The woman in the white trench coat near the pillion."

Grasping his chin, Ely watched as the images moved forward showing the time progress. At three minutes and forty-five seconds, he saw the final event. The woman in question had accidentally been knocked off the train platform and in front of the oncoming train.

"Who was she?"

"Erin Gilbert. Astrophysicist — specializing in Helioseismology." Foster smiled, cocking his eyebrow. "Acoustic pressure waves in the sun."

"Intriguing. Who is the closest operative?"

"That's the redline, right? I'll be getting off work about six blocks away right about then," Jeremiah interjected.

Jeremiah Jimenez's job as a bicycling deliveryman had a lot of the versatility and flexibility they needed. For a slim man of six feet, he had no problem whipping around the city on two wheels in his younger years. His light Hispanic skin, dark brown eyes, and long dark brown dreadlocks had the ladies chasing him even in the chaotic world they lived in now.

"Foster, open the Nexus portal. Let's send Melanie the order."

One by one, everyone filed out of the room. They all knew he liked to speak to

Melanie alone. It had been five years since he'd sent her back — five years of pain and torture — and he'd do it all over again. Everything depended on the mission succeeding.

## ~2012~

The four walls of Melanie's computer lab had never felt so constricting as she waited for the ping from the nanobot monitoring computer. It had been eighteen hours since she'd met with Ely in the coffee shop and still the nanobots hadn't activated. Everything over the last five years had led up to this moment. She couldn't go through it again.

Melanie's attention diverted three monitors down. The Sentinels were reaching out. A new mission was coming in. She slipped into the chair in front of the screen.

**2045: New recruit status?**

Melanie sighed before answering. She had a feeling she knew who was asking.

*2012: No update at this time.*

**2045: Time remaining?**

She didn't need to check the clock on the wall behind her. The ticking sound mocked her by the second.

*2012: 5 hours 54 minutes.*

The delayed response had her second guessing her first assumption to whom she was speaking with until it finally came in.

**2045: Try again.**

Melanie shook her head. That wasn't part of the deal.

*2012: Mission details.*

**2045: Live motion mission for
Jeremiah one hour
Redline – JFK/UMass Station
The woman in the white trench coat
Near the pillion on the platform
Three minutes and forty-five seconds
into video feed.**

This was always the hardest part, watching the disjointed images that led up to whenever needed changing. The woman in the white trench coat was tall and had long curly dark brown hair. She stood with her back toward the rails reading her newspaper, oblivious to what was happening around her. For a few seconds, nothing happened out of the ordinary. The crowd shifted and adjusted as new commuters arrived and merged into the train station.

Melanie cringed, looking away, and the woman's body crumpled and fell onto the track a second before the train rumbled by. It was easy to see no one meant to knock her off. The overcrowded platform, coupled with her proximity to the edge, was her downfall. Whoever she'd be, whatever she'd do, and for whatever reason they'd been necessary, the

Sentinels felt she could be of use in the future. That made her priority.

*2012: Received.*
**2045: Be happy.**
*2012: Be safe.*

They'd always ended their transmissions the same way for five years. Things were no different now than they were when she'd left. Ignoring the tear that had slipped down her cheek, she typed the coded message into her watch to Jeremiah with the time and location of his next assignment. It only took a minute to receive his affirmative confirmation in reply.

There was nothing left for her to do except wait for Ely to make his final decision. If his answer was no now, would it change how the future unfolded? Would he still be her savior in her time of need as a child? Too many questions and uncertainties and not enough answers.

# Melting the Snow

# Chapter Three

## 2012

# Into the Rabbit Hole We Go

Ely paced his small second floor in South Boston. The two vials Melanie had given him laid on the old, worn tabletop in the kitchen. He had just under an hour left to make his decision. The clock was ticking. There hadn't been a single moment in his day that didn't consist of the choice before him. Wailing sounds of a distant police cruiser's sirens filled the apartment. If he chose right, he could be more than just a mechanic; he could help people. His brother-in-law helped people for living. B-dog went from a gangbanger to a paramedic in a year. Now, he and Julie were expecting a baby in March. If one small choice like that could change their world, why couldn't it change Ely's?

Ely walked into the kitchen, snatching up both illuminated vials in his hands. There really was no choice. He put the red one back on the table and opened the green vial. Closing his eyes, he tossed it back like a shot of booze. The bitter taste lingered on his taste buds. Still, he didn't feeling any different. Maybe he'd taken the wrong one? A cynical laugh rushed out. Maybe Melanie was lying . . .

## ~2045~

"Oh — God!" A wave of pain washed over Ely like he'd never experienced before.

Salvador grabbed Ely's arm and draped it over his shoulders, hoisting his body upright against his own. "What is it? The nanobotics?"

"Yes!" Ely screeched with his pain clear in his voice. "I've accepted! I can feel them!"

Half-dragging Ely down the hall, Salvador moved them toward Ely's quarters. "You have to lie down; the pain will subside in a few hours. It's going to hurt you more as the changes catches up with you. Your younger self has it easier."

When the guard saw them approaching, he opened the door and helped Salvador pull Ely inside to his bed. "Was it this bad for you?"

"Yes, for the first few hours it's the hardest. The nanobots merge with your blood cells and transform your DNA at the cellular level. For us, it's more painful because in the past it was done over time. But now, it's an instantaneous result. Right now, your younger self is probably sleeping through it, not even realizing it has begun. The gradual change will be unnoticeable for him. You, on the other hand, will be able to pile-drive your guard immediately."

"If I could stand without my knees buckling," Ely ground through his clenched teeth. "Get my mind off the pain. How did Erin Gilbert's re-assimilation go? Any residual time ripples?"

Before the pain had set in, Ely had been headed back to the Nexus to check on that current situation.

Salvador sighed before answering, "One. A major one at that."

"What?" Ely snapped, pulling his blanket over his legs.

"It would seem she took a shining to Jeremiah and he returned it."

"Meaning?"

"After he saved her, he took her to dinner, which ended with — well . . . Jeremiah was always unattached, so this caught us off guard."

"Great, how did that play out in the timeline? So where is she in the here and now?"

"She's his wife and protected. They also had twins. A daughter and a son, both are married with families living in Salvation."

"Did he remember any of it?"

"Yes, crippled him with a migraine for an hour as the memories merged. From what we have gathered, even though he was under the protection of the continuum capsule shielding, he lived through it with her, so he retained those memories."

Ely involuntarily shivered from the nano modification effects. "So if we change a timeline in which we don't live through, we will only retain the memories we already have? Not the altered?"

Salvador pulled up a chair and sat with his friend. "That is the consensus. And all our stored video and audio is still safe. We now have two copies of Erin's incident: the original, and the one in which Jeremiah saves her."

"Salvador, what if I can't remember Melanie's early years anymore?" Ely gasped.

Fear welled in his chest at the realization. He'd held onto those memories the tightest for as long he could remember. He couldn't lose those now.

"Ely, you knew if she succeeded and diverted the future, her existence in the past would be uncertain. There is no way to know what will happen to her. If the event doesn't happen, there will be no one to send her back. She understood this before she accepted your judgment. Did you ever consider what she wanted before you sent her back?"

Ely thrashed in his bed, his flesh feeling ready to ignite from the pain radiating below his skin. "I did and it's why I sent her back, so she could have everything I couldn't give her. I just wanted her to have . . ."

"Better than you?"

"Better than what I had to offer her. I know she hates me for it, and I'm okay with that."

Salvador grasped Ely's hand in support. "You raised her. She loved you."

"She got over my betrayal a long time ago."

## ~2012~

Ely arrived at the gym a few minutes earlier than usual. After nothing happened the night before, he crashed early. A good night sleep had him up and raring to go. Salvador stood, leaning against his 2009 red Ford Explorer in the parking lot behind the gym. The only light came from a small lamp over the back door, leaving the rest of the lot completely dark. Since there were no other cars, Ely pulled up and parked next to Salvador.

Before he could grab his bag, Salvador's laugh stopped him cold. "You won't be needing that this morning. I am taking you to Melanie."

Shaking his head, Ely smiled. "She suckered you, too? Whatever was in the vial, it didn't work."

"It did, or else I wouldn't be here dragging your sorry ass to headquarters at zero-dark-thirty in the morning. Christ — the birds aren't even up yet. Now save your crap and get in the car." Without waiting for a sarcastic retort, Salvador climbed into his truck and started the engine.

For the first time since he'd swallowed the cocktail, Ely felt excited. He jogged around the SUV and hopped in grinning like an idiot. "So, MIT, right?"

Salvador slammed the car into drive, sneering, "Yeah."

~*~*~

By the time they'd parked at MIT, Ely was ready to jump out of his own skin. He couldn't explain the building excitement throughout the ride. All he knew was his life was about to change. A change he eagerly wanted.

"Pay attention, you don't get the tour again," Salvador called, hopping out and walking ahead. He stopped at a metal door secured by a strange box-like device. "It's a fingerprint scanner. Put your index finger on it." He nodded to Ely to comply.

Ely did as he instructed, asking, "Are we programming it?"

Salvador didn't have to answer when the lock clicked open, but that didn't stop him from teasing Ely. "You've been in the system for years, bonehead."

"What happens if the power goes out?" The thirst to know more overtook Ely.

"This lab was built specially to suit the Sentinels' needs. That's why it's not connected to any other structures on campus. The power, water — everything runs independently."

Looking around, it didn't escape Ely's attention that the only thing on the ground floor where the mechanical necessities. Salvador waved his hand to a metal staircase leading down.

"Into the rabbit hole." He laughed and turned, going back out the way he came.

"Ready or not — here I come," Ely mumbled to himself as he took his first step.

His footfalls clambered and echoed off the concrete walls surround the stairs. If Melanie didn't know he was coming before, she would now.

"You'll need to work on your stealth." Melanie cocked her slim eyebrow at him when he skipped the last step and landed with a thud at the bottom.

Ely grinned. She looked good in pants the day before, but in a tight, black, pencil skirt and sheer white blouse, she looked down-right hot.

"What can I say? I like to make grand entrances."

Melanie knew that cocky attitude all too well. "Get over it. Our end of the Nexus is this way."

She'd barely slept after the nano monitor had finally chimed. Ely had cut it close. Too close for her comfort. Salvador was already on his way over to his apartment to try to persuade him when the nanobots set off the warnings. Though she'd said she wouldn't reach out to Ely again, that didn't mean she didn't have a backup plan.

The Sentinels had spent five years planning and stockpiling before she could be sent back, she wouldn't risk not having every avenue covered. It was one of the reasons Ely wasn't the first one approached. He never would have accepted without the others as proof.

"Wow — how many computers do you have here?"

Melanie couldn't help but smile. "That's right. You don't even have one at home. The Nexus is comprised of twenty-two interlocking interfaces shielded by a continuum capsule. What that means is the information stored there is in neither time continuum so that it can't be corrupted when changes are made. Since I'm not a scientist, and neither are you, it's easiest to put as: it's an electrical sphere that surrounds the core where time has no influence."

"Does your timeline shift with each change made?"

"Yes, on the outside, but not inside the

Nexus. It's shielded in a continuum capsule as well."

"Is it instantaneous?"

"Yes, time ripples are the biggest problems. Once something changes here, the outward flow stretches through time to reflect the change that follows."

"So what        did you come to fix?"

"It doesn't work that way, Ely. I'm the only one who knows the main event. With any luck, the minor corrections we're making won't make it necessary for anyone else to know besides me. So for now it stays that way."

"Not a very trusting group."

"We have a good reason not to be. For now, just worry about getting yourself ready. For starters," Melanie held up a watch that matched hers, "you'll need this. Everyone has one and they're all connected. Your messages will all start with either live or frozen to let you know the type of motion involved. Second line of the message is the location, followed by the time and countdown to the mission. Don't mess up. I will be waiting to hear a confirmation that the mission message was received by you and again once it's completed. Other than that, contact between the team is kept to a minimum."

Her eyes met his when his fingers grazed hers as he grasped the cool metal. For a split second, she could almost see the man she once knew: the man who raised her, who would do anything for her, who wouldn't send her away. Too many nights she wondered what happened to him. Now she didn't want to care where he'd gone. She had her own private hell to survive.

"What, no bedtime stories?" Hearing Ely mimic her words from their meeting had Melanie swallowing back her retort.

She turned toward the computers. "Those days are long over for me."

Ely slipped into a seat in front of one of the monitors, putting the watch on the desk. "Why don't I feel any different yet?"

"You won't notice it. The proof is in the data. It's on this one." Melanie pointed to the nanobotic monitoring interface. "See the progress percentage bar here. It's already at twenty-five percent. So far, the bots have merged with your blood cells on a cellular level and have begun to modify your DNA. Within a week, they'll have completed their modifications. As I said before: you won't be a superhero, but you will be able to withstand more than most. Let's get this on before you forget it." Melanie whisked the communicator off the desk.

Ely asked, exposing his left wrist, "What's it made of?"

"Titanium and a crystalonic interface," she explained, sealing the latching.

"So my guess was partially right. It's a

mini computer?" Ely smirked and twisted his wrist, testing the feel of his link.

"Yes. Quinn was able to replicate mine with the five crystalonic sheers I brought with me. He's the lab head here who will be a Sentinel in the future. I told you a little about him at our meeting. Don't let anything happen to the link. There are only six of these at the moment and all of them are or will be attached to a Sentinel. Each link forms a distinct connection to the nanobots in your system."

"Then you're a Sentinel as well?"

"No, I work for them," Melanie huffed.

She knew the onslaught of questions needed to be answered, that didn't mean she wanted to be the one to answer them. With all the resentment she harbored toward him for sending her back, being his handler would be trying at best.

"How will I read the coded symbols?"

"The bots will do it for you internally."

"That's cool. So I have to ask: since you're from the future, where's the ray guns, and all the high tech toys everyone said we'd have?"

"We weren't sure what would withstand the journey through the portal, so I traveled light. Some of the technology in one of the operating systems to the terminal had been corrupted, but was easily replaced once I uplinked with the Nexus. The fabric of my clothes barely held together." Melanie laughed, remembering how her clothes had disintegrated like tissue paper when she tried to take them off.

"Why not just go through and get more?"

"It was a one way ticket. It took all the compounds we could scrounge to get enough to send me. There are no more. They've been looking; they're just depleted."

"Can't you get them here or buy more?"

"We don't use paper money in the future, so we had to gather up as many precious stones as we could for me to convert into cash here. I've been turning them over slowly so not to draw any attention."

"How do you pay for things like food and clothes?"

"Inside Salvation, everyone has a central banking account of sorts that is accessed by a combination fingerprint and DNA scanner."

"Salvation?"

"That's the name of the city built around what is now known as MIT."

"Why did Salvador say I'd been in the system for years?"

"In the future, you're a member of the Order as you are now, hence you've been in the system since the moment the system here became live."

"I guess that makes sense. It's just weird hearing you talking about me in the futuristic sense. You already know me and I know nothing about you. Hey, what's behind those doors? Why are they dead-bolted?"

Melanie gladly allowed him to shift the topic away. "Those rooms are in case all else fails and the event happens anyways. Everyone will report here. The Head Sentinel had them built as a precaution. No amount of reassurance had persuaded him otherwise. He's a little headstrong."

"Who is he?" Ely pushed the wrong button.

"There will be time for that later. For now, we need to worry about getting you up to speed here. It would be better if you didn't work out at the gym this week. Your physical adjustments are a little unstable at the moment."

"I can't just sit around. I'll go crazy."

"You don't have to. There is a gym here. At least I'd be able to watch your progress, and should you slip up," Melanie laughed with a tad of sarcasm in her tone, "no one would see it."

"I'll take it there have been slips?" he grumbled.

Ely grinned at her the way he used to in the old days, causing her expression to fall and forcing her to put back up the walls of separation she'd carefully built. Too much time had passed to allow herself to get close to anyone who would get in the way of her achieving her goal. The sacrifices made came at too high of a price tag to jeopardize the ultimate outcome.

"Yeah, a couple. Anyways, the rest of the team will be here in less than an hour if you want to hang around."

"Morning, Mel," Salvador called as he trampled down the stairs.

Thankful for the distraction, she turned her back on Ely and headed to her desk in the corner. "It's clear. Hopefully you brought coffee?"

"Don't I always?" His chuckled ricocheted off the walls.

"Hey, Ely. How did it go?"

"Great. I think she hates me."

"I don't doubt that." Salvador placed the coffee cup on the desk in front of his boss with a wink.

For him, Melanie shared a genuine smile, but she spoke to Ely. "He'll show you to the workout room."

"Come on before she kicks your ass for fun."

Silently following Salvador through the underground, concrete, and metallic pipelined corridors, Ely discovered it was more of a mini complex. They passed a small kitchen, lounge, library, and finally found the gym.

"We'll start on the heavy bag. You won't need your gloves much nowadays." Salvador steadied the bag for the coming onslaught. They'd done this before at Blackie's.

Shrugging, Ely nodded and approached the long black leather bag. "Sal, we've known each other for a few years. Feel like sharing why she can't stand me?" he asked after his first swing, savoring the burn in his muscles.

"Nope. She'll tell if she wants you to know."

Frustration bubbled to the surface. "Come on! Did I steal her kitten or something? She said I brought her to the Sentinels."

"You did." Salvador always knew how to keep his cool, and it always irked Ely to no end.

Ely couldn't explain why he needed to know more about Melanie. He just knew there was more that they weren't telling him. Those questions craved to be answered. "Did I just abandon her there or something?"

Cocking his brow, Sal bumped Ely with the bag, provoking him. "Now does that sound like something you'd do?"

He threw a left hook with his reply. "No. Then what?"

"Ask her," Sal hissed from the impact.

Before he could recover, Ely threw an upper jab. "Will she tell me?"

He smiled when Sal's footing slipped a fraction. "Doubt it."

"You're a big help." Ely hammered the bag with a combination of shots.

Sal gave the bag one last heave toward

Ely, barely missing him. "My pleasure."

Before Ely could question him more, two new team members entered the room. "Oh joy, Ely finally joined."

"Ely, this is Jeremiah Jimenez and that's Foster Kane."

"Hey." He reached out and shook both their hands. Neither looked overly impressed to be meeting him.

"Well, how long before B-Dog joins?" Foster finally asked, setting the treadmill to high.

Ely looked back to Sal. "My brother-in-law?"

"Yep. He's the last one." Sal laughed, slapping him on the back.

"Damn. Melanie never mentioned him." Again, more questions than answers.

"You're still on the need to know, and you don't need to know," Jeremiah heckled as he moved into position behind the heavy bag.

For the next hour, Ely seemed to be the butt of all jokes that he didn't understand. By the time he stormed out the door and into the parking lot, he was beyond frustrated and ready to walk away from the Sentinels and anything else to do with them.

A whisper stopped him in his tracks. "Ely, don't do it."

"Why not, Melanie?" he snapped without turning back. "Everyone here — with the exception of Sal — hates me, so give me one reason why I should stay."

His tense shoulder relaxed under her warm hand. "It won't always be this way."

"What do I do in the future that turns everyone against me?"

A chill ghosted over his skin when her hand fell away. "You have it wrong. Elysian the Heroic, you'll earn their loyalty with a strength none have ever seen. In the future, we'd die for you."

# Melting the Snow

# Chapter Four

## 2012

# Strength from the Innocent

Melanie's final words rattled around Ely's mind for days after he left MIT. He'd refused to go back until he could square away his hurt feelings over the way they'd treated him, and why it seem to matter to him. How people he didn't even know felt about him had never mattered to Ely. So why did it now? Or did it have something to with Melanie? Where the guys just teased him, most of the time she couldn't hide her hatred of him, but then she'd flip-flop and show a softer side as she had when they last parted ways.

Ely had stayed away from Blackie's Boxing Gym also, and he continued to work out alone as suggested. The team had yet to contact him. Always the lone wolf it would seem.

He couldn't deny the physical improvements. He could now run a mile in three and half minutes. That would beat the world record, but he was pretty sure that would count as a slip up if anyone had caught him.

Concealed under the hood of his black sweatshirt, Ely watched the people of the city moving around without noticing him perched above them. An overcast day mimicked his mood. Yet the solace of standing in an alcove of the Trinity Church in Copley Square filled him with peace.

When his watch hummed, a nest of pigeons took flight. That couldn't be a good sign. Lifting his sleeve, he read the message.

**URGENT - First attempt failed
Live motion
Stop Black Mercedes collision with
white delivery truck
Corner of Nassau Street and Pine
Street
7:47A.M. 3:31:01**

All conscious thought and worry fled his mind. This was what Ely had waited for. The moment had arrived when he'd prove himself, not just to the team, but to the person who mattered most: himself. Ely dropped to the ground like it had been mere feet instead of two stories. Gracefully, his feet touched down and he took off running. Careful not to be seen, he took a creative route to the destination.

Three buildings down, he slipped to the back and scrambled up a fire escape. Adrenalin coursed through his veins as a roar begged to rip from his mouth. After reaching the rooftop, he let loose and charged from one to the next, flying over the gaps. Granted, he wasn't a superhero, but he felt like one. At the end of the block, he dropped back to the ground level via another set of fire escapes.

Somersaulting over a wrought iron fence, Ely pushed himself harder with only a minute left until the deadline. Jumping and flipping, he dropped down two flights of stone staircases, only to have to skirt and leap up match sets on the other side of the water fountain. Ely pushed forward by dodging and weaving through the cars in the street until he reached the corner of Broad Street and Nassau Street before he was forced to veer onto the sidewalk. He knew it was rude to shove those walking on the sidewalk that got in the way, but it was a small sacrifice. The lights at the corner of Pine Street were red, blocking the black Mercedes from pulling away. That worked in his favor as he threw himself onto the hood, preventing the driver from moving when the white pickup barreled through the intersection.

It took a second for Ely to look up and see the driver; once he did, he couldn't believe what he saw: auburn hair and gray eyes. The eyes were an exact match. She looked back, her fear plainly written on her face. A small child cried in the back seat, drawing her attention away for a split second. It wasn't

Melanie, but an educated guess: Melanie's mother. His focus landed on the girl in the car seat.

"Melanie?" he whispered in disbelief.

Rage raced through his veins and he punched the car hood in frustration. His breaths rushed out in panted huffs.

Had he just imagined the resemblance?

The mother cried into her hands. Ely used that moment to disappear into the crowd that had gathered at the corner. He glanced up at the bridge that crossed over the road to see Foster, Salvador, and Jeremiah staring back at him as they stood inside the glass enclosure. He was just about to turn away when Foster saluted and turned first. The rest followed suit and disappeared.

~*~*~

Work had been hell after Ely's first mission. The last place he wanted to be was cooped up in a garage working on cars he didn't own. On the way home, he detoured and grabbed a six pack of Budweiser. After long days, Ely often sought refuge on the rooftop to his apartment building, even in the cold weather. Ely sat in an old, worn lawn chair. The city hummed with life around, completely unaware of his presence. Sighing, he cracked open the bottle of beer.

"That would be a bad idea." Melanie

giggled, coming up behind him.

"I'll live with the hangover. I'm a big boy now." He laughed before chugging the entire bottle. No sooner had Ely gulped down the last mouthful, his stomach churned painfully.

"It's not the hangover you need to worry about. The nanobotics aren't fond of alcohol," Melanie stated as he doubled over, clutching his stomach as it threatened to spill everything he'd ingested back out. "Give in to it, Ely. It's the only way."

"No!"

"Why not?" Melanie knelt beside him, hesitantly wrapping her arm around his shoulder.

Without thinking, he admitted the truth. "I won't be weak."

"You're not weak, Ely, far from it. You'll do things most men can't." He wanted to believe her. Something deep inside held him back.

"Tell me why you hate me? What did I do to you?"

Something in her gray eyes softened for a brief moment, then in a blink, it was gone again. "Later. Let's handle this first, okay?"

"No, now!" Ely chucked the bottle across the roof, causing it to shatter against the side wall. "Tell me, so I don't make the same mistake!" Even to Ely it sounded whiney.

He watched her bite her lip as she mulled

it over. Finally she closed her eyes and granted his wish. "You sent me back in time. I'm sorry; it's not something I can easily forgive, Ely." When her eyes popped open again, the fire had returned. "You stole everything from me and sent me here to be alone. That's why I hate you."

Melanie tried to pull her hand away, but Ely was quicker. The stunned look on her delicate features spoke volumes of her lack of personal contact. "Did I know you didn't want the mission?"

"You know now, and knew then. As you see, I am still here." She tried to pull away, but Ely held tight. "So you still made the same decision to send me here."

Ely decided to shift tactics. "Who did I save today?"

It worked, and Melanie suddenly took the defensive posture he hoped for. "I don't know. The message didn't come with any video or names. I don't have the pleasure of questioning my bosses. They send the orders; my job is to pass them along."

She shivered when he pulled her closer. "What happened after I brought you back?"

"Ely . . ."

"Answer me! You said: 'It was one of my favorite bedtime stories.' When you knew what I was thinking in the coffee shop. Did we stay together after we returned?" he pushed for more details.

"Yes, you raised me in the Matrix — that's underground portion of Salvation — until I was of legal age," Melanie answered, but still struggled to free herself.

He searched her eyes. "There's more that you're not telling me."

"Yes." Her reply was a mere whisper.

"Why hold back?"

Melanie knew why. She'd always known. After begging and pleading not to be sent away, the answer was clear. "It won't change anything." With that, she managed to rip her arm away from Ely.

She spun on her heel and headed for the door to the stairs, hearing Ely calling out to her. "You don't know that!"

"Yes, I do!" she laughed, waving her hand over her head as she disappeared through the doorway.

The sounds of Ely retching up the booze started after just three steps. It was rather gratifying. He should have heeded her warning. Then again, she had deliberately left out that minor detail in her briefing, knowing he'd be paying for it eventually.

"You're evil, Melanie," Salvador chided from the landing below.

She shrugged and grinned. "He deserves it."

"No one deserves that. The nanobotics have the alarms at headquarters going ballistic," he retorted, looking up.

Shaking her head, she stopped and crossed her arms over her chest. "How did you know to come here anyways?"

Salvador tapped his link. "They overrode it, and sent me with a message. You'll have to answer to *him* when you get back."

"*Great*. What's the message?"

"Have fun cleaning him up."

"You're not serious!" She stomped her foot.

"I'm here to ensure you stay and fix your mess. Then I'm to go back to headquarters and take your watch while you're here with him."

This wasn't something Melanie was looking forward to, or having to explain it to the head of the Sentinel Order why she'd done it. She should have known she'd get caught. They saw everything. Nothing was sacred or private with them. The nanobotics sold her out and reported Ely's alcohol absorption, and by association, her failure to stop him or warn him of its affects.

Melanie and Ely would have a long night of cleansing ahead of them, then it still wasn't over. Thanks to Ely keeping the unwanted liquor in for as long as he did, the nanos would continue to be confused for at least another twenty-four hours until they managed to burn all the residual traces off. To the bots, this equaled a massive infection that needed to be terminated without prejudice. That meant they would massively raise his temperature.

"I can't be trapped alone with him for all that time. Please, Salvador?" she begged for some form of mercy.

"You've made your bed, now lay in it." He nodded toward the sounds of Ely gagging above.

Melanie huffed. "This is cruel and unusual punishment."

"I'll be sure to tell your husband you said that. Night, Melanie."

Before she could say anything in reply, he left her standing in the stairwell gawking at his backside. The man was just plain mean. Maybe it was all men . . .

Surrendering to her fate, Melanie stomped back up the stairs to see Ely kneeling over a puddle of his own vomit. Her life officially sucked at the moment; well, it always did.

"Come on, you idiot. Let's get you inside and cleaned up."

"Melanie, I don't want you to hate me," he slurred into her neck as she wrapped her arms around Ely.

"I know."

Melanie did know, but it wouldn't — couldn't — be allowed to change her mission. The future couldn't happen. She'd fight and conquer it with her dying breath before she'd relive that life again. Ely had built the best life for her he could. Sadly, it was filled with pain and heartbreak. He said she'd find the happiness the future had denied her; he lied. It had been far worse in the past.

Ely staggered to his feet and leaned against Melanie. As she'd led the way down the stairs, she remembered all the times they'd do the simple things like share a meal or swap stories after a hard day's work. Those were the closest ones to happy memories she had now.

By the time they reached his apartment, Melanie was practically dragging Ely. He'd also developed a nasty case of the chuckles. Everything seemed funny to him, even the way she opened his door. It was rather annoying.

Melanie led Ely into his bed and went to retrieve a cool, wet washcloth from the bathroom.

"Melanie?"

"I'm here, Ely."

"I thought you left me again." His head lolled on the pillow.

She sat on the bed to apply the cloth to his forehead. As tempting as it was, she bit back her nasty retort. "No, your body is rejecting the alcohol. The bots are raising your temperature to burn off the booze."

"I didn't know," he mumbled. "I saw you there, you know."

Melanie sighed, knowing hallucinations

were part of the package deal with this situation. "That was my fault, which I am now paying penance for."

"I forgive you."

She tried several times to reply. Each time her words stuck in her throat. If only it were that easy.

"I'm hot."

Before Melanie could stop him, Ely tore off his white T-shirt. That would make the night a whole lot longer. As if it couldn't get worse, he pushed off his gray sweatpants, too. Laying there in his briefs, he was still sweating. The tiny beads could be seen without any effort. She made several trips to refresh the washcloth. Each time she left his side, he called out to her.

Just after two o'clock, Melanie's eyes started to droop. It had been a long day for her as well. When Ely wrapped around her and snuggled, she didn't resist, and instead she let him pull her down onto the bed. His blazing, slick skin covered her like a heated blanket.

~*~*~

A warm breeze washed over Melanie's face a second before something moist touched her lips. Lost in the fatigue and the sleepy haze, she instinctively licked them. Something returned the favor with a soft humming sound. The heated, brushing caresses became more urgent and harder to deny. Every nerve ending in her body electrified. Forgotten cravings buried deep in her soul clawed their way to the surface. Waves of heated pressure moved over her, threatening to ignite her flesh. Her hands reached out and found the hard yet soft skin that was causing the sensations. It was heaven and hell.

Melanie almost forgot to fight the warming feelings brewing in her body. Almost being the keyword. Her sleepy mind jarred awake.

The delicious kisses came to an abrupt halt when Melanie slapped Ely square across the cheek. From the dazed and glazed over look in his eyes, he had no idea what was happening at the time. She knew. The 104 fever burning within his body was wreaking havoc on his mind. Forcing a smile on her face, she cupped his cheeks and nodded. He relaxed against her as she held him close again.

Chances were Ely would never remember what had happened, but her heart would. That one moment would forever be frozen in time there. Hidden in a place where only she could feel and hold it safe.

For hours, Melanie tried to fight the fever when finally more was needed. "You need a shower, Ely."

Again, Melanie nearly carried Ely to get him to the bathroom. With one arm, she held him up while she started the shower. Since he'd shed most of his clothes, that part was easy enough.

"It's cold." His teeth chattered as he stepped in.

Melanie stripped off her boots and clothes while Ely shivered in the corner. "You actually have to let the water touch you for this to work."

"I — I can't — I can't stand up," Ely sputtered, slipping down the wall and crumbling to a heap on the bottom.

Melanie slipped into the tub bottom behind Ely, pulling his limp body backward to rest against her chest. "I've got you. Just let the water lower your temperature."

"Tell me what the future is like."

"Salvation is not so bad. We've rebuilt it. But the wastelands are ugly and dangerous. Nature took back what it wanted. Without the government, people went crazy. Gangs of nomads control the roads. The highways are littered with abandoned cars and over-turned trucks. Most of the high-rise buildings were reduced to rubble. There were a lot of fires after the . . . planes fell from the sky when they ran out of gas."

"Sounds scary. It's no wonder you want to change it. Is that how you lost your parents?"

"Yeah, there's a group of renegades that

control the outer boroughs with terror. The Arch Angels like to travel by motorcycles. They found us one day when we were searching for food." A tear slipped from her cheek at the memory of her parents. "They killed them right in front of me. They'd have killed me, too, if it weren't for the promise of a meal coming along. A six-point buck dashed down the road and they took off after it. I didn't hang around and wait for them to come back."

His eyes sparkled when he looked up. "You're beautiful."

"What?" Melanie laughed.

"I know you're used to the fathering me from your time, but I'm not him — well, not yet anyways. Right now — I'm just a man who thinks you're beautiful."

"You're hallucinating from the fever. No worries, tomorrow you'll be an ass again."

Ely turned in her lap, grabbing her right, bra-clad breast. "Since it's not real, then this is okay."

Before Melanie could correct him, he crushed his lips to hers. This time she didn't need to stop him. The fatigue won out and his hand fell away.

"Melanie," Ely sighed her name into her neck.

"We need to get you back to bed."

She managed to push him up enough to shut off the water before it ran cold. That would have shocked his system to the extreme. With him draped around her, Melanie dragged him back to his bed where she dried him off before she laid him back between his sheets. The few seconds she'd seen him naked had awakened the forgotten woman in her. There had been too many years of empty nights. The door to her husband had been closed the moment she left her time. There was no way back to him now. They'd both accepted that a long time ago.

Melanie borrowed one of Ely's T-shirts and crawled in to comfort him as best as she could. He kept her awake for the rest of the night when he would kiss her or lap at her neck. Still, she refused to let go of her grasp on him. Her body hung on the edge of excitement with each grind of his form against her. By the time the late afternoon rays of light filtered in through the window, his temperature had receded, but it still wasn't back to normal.

"You're still here?"

"Yeah, you didn't make it easy."

Melanie tried to roll away only to be pulled flush against his body so their faces were inches apart. His eyes burned with emotions.

"You hate me enough to try to kill me?"

"Not kill. I just wanted to knock you down a notch." She shook her head. "It's stupid really. I'm going to have my ass handed to me for it, too. I wanted revenge, but it didn't work. Watching you suffer, hearing you ramble, seeing you so weak, you're not the one I want to punish."

"You don't have to worry about me coming anywhere near you. Get your stuff and get out."

"Ely . . ."

"No, Melanie. I tried to be friends. My repayment was . . . just get out." Instead of waiting for her to move, he rolled away and left her laying there shocked. "I'll do my missions, I'll save your future, but that's where *we* end." Yanking on his jeans, he turned his back on her.

"Wait, Ely —" She bounced up, trying to grab his arm.

He spun, his hand flying up. "No! You don't have the right to call me Ely. That's reserved for my friends. You call me Elysian."

Her heart broke at his tone. He'd never spoken so harshly to her. "Please, it was wrong," she pleaded.

"You bet your ass it was." Ely backhanded everything on his end table onto the floor. "You made your bed, now sleep in it, sweetheart. I'm taking a shower, be gone when I get out."

Hopelessness filled her soul as he stormed away and slammed the door behind him. After all the years she'd known him, Ely had never been that mad at anyone, especially her. Melanie scrambled from the bed and froze. Her clothes and boots were on the bathroom floor. In a single moment, she'd ruined everything. Even if they'd corrected the future, her life would be as it was now. Miserable.

# Melting the Snow

# Chapter Five

## 2012

## A Living Hell

Reluctantly, Ely walked out of the dressing room at Blackie's two weeks after the blowout with Melanie. He'd deliberately avoided headquarters and the team. Their sympathy or aggressions he didn't need or want. Ely had no idea how much they knew about what had happen — he didn't care.

Since that day, Ely had been screwed up in the head too much to be around too many people. Work was hard enough. Rafe at least left him to his repairs. A few missions had come through, each was completed and dismissed. Other than that, he avoided everyone.

It hurt more than his head to think of Melanie's betrayal. Deep down, it hurt his heart, too. He couldn't explain why. They hadn't been that close, though he had held out hopes they could be. He knew she only saw him as the father figure from the future, but he saw her as a woman he could love one day if he could ever get past her Icy Queen act. It never occurred to him she'd be capable of being that cruel or dangerous.

"Good, you're gloved. Get in the ring." Ely

tensed at Salvador's voice from the far wall.

"Why are you here?"

"You're the only one able to withstand my *sparring* and vice versa. So let's go."

Without waiting for his retort, Sal jumped up onto the mat platform and under the ropes. Bouncing on his feet, he took a few jabs at the air while he waited for Ely to join him. Ely shook it off and did the same. The two met in the center and slipped in their mouth pieces before tapping their gloves.

At first the two danced around barely landing any strikes. That all changed soon enough.

"Look, I don't know what happened after I left you and Melanie on the roof," Sal garbled, landing a solid left hook against Ely's jaw. "But I do know how the Order laid into her, not that she needed it." Ely dodged the right Sal swung next. "Whatever you said, or did, had already done a number on her."

Sal should have kept his mouth shut. Ely let loose with a left, right, left combination. All three body shots landed in Sal's midsection. "She's the one who tried to kill me."

The next two retaliation strikes from Sal were quick, but not as effective. "Alcohol wouldn't kill you. It just hurts like hell."

"It was still a bitch move." Ely's uppercut to Sal's jaw knocked his mouth guard out of his mouth and him to the mat.

"That it was," Sal panted.

Heaving to catch his breath, Ely nodded, looking down and offering a glove up. "So is that why you're here? To get me to forgive her or some shit?"

"Nope, like I said: I just wanted someone to knock gloves with. What happens between you two is just that — between you two. I will tell you though; she's really messed up right now. I've never seen Melanie cry. She stormed into headquarters that day in tears, rambling about time ripples in the fabric of time and how she'd ruined everything. After the Order ripped into her, I believe her."

Ely's interest was piqued against his wishes. "What do you mean?"

"Tear enough holes in the fabric of time and some things can't be fixed. We're very careful with what we fix. Whatever happened with you wasn't a fix it, it undid some major things in the timeline from what I gather. Melanie refused to tell me what, but they had to be huge. She's also been sick since that night."

"Sick how?" he asked, dropping out of the ring.

"Her hands shake a lot, she's off balance like she's dizzy, and she's acting weird, like taking down all the pictures of her at headquarters." He shrugged after dropping down to the floor behind Ely.

"Did you tell the Sentinels?"

Sal laughed. "We don't talk to them. They have the ability to override our links, not the other way around." He checked his link. "Hey, I gotta run. Thanks for the workout. Tomorrow?"

"Yeah. Sounds good."

Maybe Ely was ready to start off slowly. One on one was a good place to begin. He still had no idea what to do about Melanie.

Her betrayal had cut so deep that he had no idea where to begin the healing process to get them back to being on talking terms, never mind being friends. Hearing she was unwell didn't sit easily with him though.

For the next week Sal and Ely continued to meet daily and workout. By the end of the week, Jeremiah joined in the mix. Nothing more was said about Melanie, which suited Ely fine. By the end of the next week, Foster began the early morning boxing club.

Ely had to wonder how Melanie felt about losing her coffee delivery now that they all worked out together away from headquarters.

"Melanie?" Foster peeked in the computer lab.

"Morning. Long time no see. Here to work out?"

"No, we've been working out with Ely at the gym. Is everything okay with you?"

"Sure. Why do ask?" she lied, forcing a smile on her face.

The team would never see how much it

crushed her. Nothing would be okay as it stood. No matter how hard she tried to think of a way to fix the current situation, there were no solutions. Ely would never trust her again. The time ripples had already done that damage. The more time that passed, the greater the effects. She'd already begun feeling its ramifications. Much more and she'd disappear from the current timeline altogether. Her grasp on here was only mere threads. A few more snaps and she'd be gone. The altercation with Ely had already twisted their previous lives she'd remembered. Now when he finds her, he can't stand her. Their years later are strained and rough. Her heart breaks every time she remembers the new memories. They were never meant to be that way. Every night she'd sit rereading how things had once gone before the tear from her Nexus journal logs. Now she had nothing left and nothing to look forward to.

Foster smiled and shook his head. "Must be me. Okay, I'm off. Have a good day."

"You, too."

Once he'd disappeared back up the stairwell, Melanie pulled out a picture from her desk drawer of her, Sal, and Foster. She could barely recognize herself anymore in the photo. It was now overlaid with the image of Dawnna Nowlan.

She was the candidate who actually wanted the mission. She also wanted the sexual attentions of several Sentinels in the bedroom. Coincidence? Doubtful.

All the pictures of Melanie here were fading or changing. That could only mean one thing. The Order would be changing their choice of who to send back from the future. Her messing up had set it off. Left with no way to fix it, she had no real options. Once she re-assimilated back to where she belonged in the future, she'd lose everything and everyone for which she'd fought for so long.

Melanie knew nothing else in life. Her life, loves, and friends all revolved around the Sentinel Order and Salvation. If that ended — so did she.

### 2045: New Mission Melanie and Elysian Schedule to bring in B-dog
### Time Freeze display
### Car crash at the corner of Maverick Street and Geneva Street
### November 19, 2012 7:30 P.M.
*2012: Received.*

Hissing out a breath, Melanie sat back in her chair. They didn't even trust her to bring in a new recruit anymore. She couldn't help wondering how Ely would take the news of having to go with her, or the fact that they'd be bringing in his brother-in-law. Time would tell. Before she could dwell on it, she shot Ely the mission information over his link. Two days' notice would give him plenty of time to storm in and scream his refusal or he just wouldn't show up. Either way, it would be a miserable time had by all involved.

~*~*~

It didn't surprise Melanie that Ely hadn't shown up prior to the meeting date to object to the job at hand, but it did shock her that he was waiting at the location with B-dog when she arrived for the intake offer.

"Have you explained everything already?" she snipped.

"And deny you the Queen Bee status you clawed your way up to? Never." Ely stepped back, bowing and waving his hand toward her. "He's all yours. I just told him what you're about to tell him is the truth."

Just hearing the disdain in his voice felt like a vice around her soul. There was only so much a person could take, and Melanie had reached the end of her rope. Once B-dog had been brought in, her job was done. The team would be complete. They could run themselves at that point; they didn't need her.

It took less time to convince B-dog than anyone else. Once Melanie explained how it worked and he watched the accident freeze, he was sold. B-dog drank the nanos on the spot when Ely nodded that they were safe. It took less than one hour to finalize the last component that would make the correction team complete. Quinn would only be given his nanos in the event the team failed.

"That's it then, I'll see you at MIT tomorrow to receive your link." Melanie tried to reach out to shake his hand, but her tremors had her pulling back.

B-dog laughed, not noticing. "Not gonna lie, this was one weird night."

"I hear that a lot." Melanie tried her best to smile even though Ely glared at her. "Have a good night."

Ely grabbed her arm when she spun away. "Did you drive here?"

"I don't own a car. I'm a public transportation girl." She yanked her arm back.

"We'll give you a lift. Where do you live?" He called to her as she walked away.

"No need. I'll be fine."

Though she'd managed to keep her voice fine, Melanie was anything but fine. There was only one thing left to do. Now she needed to decide how. She needed a way to just disappear off the planet. Easier said than done. There could be no evidence she ever existed. The nanos could never be found. Whatever she did, they needed to be destroyed along with her body.

***

# Chapter Six

## 2045

## The Black Plague

Salvador strolled into Ely's office looking worse for the wear. "Ely, Salvation's having a new issue with the Black Plague. There were four new deaths last night."

His anger flashed at the mention of the drug that had killed so many of their citizens. It first appeared a year after Salvation had reopened its streets. The black powder came packaged in an inhaler device. Ten puffs for one hundred credits. The effects varied by person, but generally included euphoria, accelerated heart rate, excitability, hallucinations, and sometimes violence. Unfortunately, it also included those symptoms to the extreme. Death by the Black Plague was a gruesome and painful way to die.

He hissed out a long breath, laying his crystalonic pad on his desk. "I thought we'd had it beat for good. We've warned everyone about how deadly it is; still they seek it out. How did it get back in?"

"We're not sure. Someone had to have snuck it in from a recent trip outside the walls. It's a banned substance. No one here would make it."

Ely stood and looked out his high rise office window. The city below bustled with life. Overcrowding was quickly becoming a problem as they managed to spare more lives in the past. Soon they'd need to expand their walls to accommodate.

It had only been a month since his younger self had joined the team in the past, and in that time, Salvation had already gained over a thousand re-assimilated citizens and by-product families as they'd been labeled. The memory merges were easier to recognize now. It mimicked a brief moment of déjà vu and then it was cemented in place.

The Order had dealt with Melanie's lapse in judgment, but tensions in the past timeline were tenuous at best. The team itself had strengthened, but Melanie's action had put everyone on Ely's side and against her. That one tiny change had altered events leading up to her being sent back. Each Sentinel agreed; in order to correct the timeline, steps needed to be taken to correct her altered life line. For the sake of all involved, it couldn't be left as it was.

Ely keyed up the large crystalonic screen in the center of his office. Doctor Quinn's image appeared as he leaned over a corpse lying on the center metallic table.

"Report, Quinn."

"I'd say good morning, Ely, but so far, there has been nothing good about it, as you can see."

He stepped to the side to expose the facial features of one of the male victims. They'd all seen the results of the Black Plague. Thin trails of blood had dried where they ran from his nose, the corner of his mouth, eyes, and ears. The whites of his eyes were now tinted red from the broken capillaries. His veins stood bulged and black through his pale skin.

"Doesn't get any easier to see, does it?"

"No, but there is one that you do need to see. It pertains to the correction team and the time ripples from Melanie."

The screen followed Quinn as he walked to the far wall and lowered a white sheet over another table.

Ely's eyebrow tilted up in confusion. "Is that . . ."

"Yes, Dawnna Nowlan. Problem is, if you look closely, she's metamorphosing. From the Nexus's calculations, approximating from the measurements and dimensions, it's into . . . Melanie Shepherd." He croaked at the end.

Ely swallowed hard. This had been one of the concerns in the last Order session. "Understood. I'll be sure to take this news to the rest of the Order. It will need to be dealt with quickly."

"I'm sorry, Ely. It does answer why she

has yet to show up as a re-assimilated."

"Yes. I've had a few ideas on this matter. We'll handle it next." Ely refocused to the first problem at hand while still keeping his eyes trained on Dawnna's lifeless eyes. They'd already begun to shift from an amber brown to Melanie's steel gray. "So whose squad was the last one to leave our walls?"

Sal flipped through his cry-pad images. "B-dog's. They made a medicine trade run to Troika a few days ago."

Troika laid across the Charles River over what was once Back Bay, Boston. Salvation had a treaty with them: in exchange for medical supplies, they provided food from their gardening nurseries. A wasteland of destruction separated them, yet they found a way to work together.

"Quinn, anything new in their toxicology reports?" One could only hope the maker had left a fingerprint of sorts.

Quinn leaned back over the corpse as he continued to work. "No, Ely. The usual organic matters, volcanic ash mixed with LSD. Just the idea of inhaling pulverized rock and glass makes no sense to me."

"Was this batch also from Mount Ossipee?"

"Yes. It's identical to all the overdoses. Usually, even if someone follows a recipe, there is always a slight variance. Whoever made these doses made them all at once."

"Let us know if anything new comes up, Quinn. We'll check into the team."

"Will do, Ely." With a wave of his hand, the screen went blank.

It couldn't be allowed to continue. The people of Salvation needed saving once and for all. They needed to find out how it was slipping past their security. "Let's pay B-dog a visit. We need to get to the bottom of this."

Without thinking, Ely stood and headed toward the door only to be stopped by Sal. "Your cloak?"

"Right, guess it's been a while since I've been outside." He winced when he grabbed it from his seat.

Maybe it had been too long. Ely couldn't actually remember the last time he'd walked the streets, smelled the fresh air, and taken in the scenery. His days were split between his office, the Nexus, and his quarters.

"You should do it more often." Sal studied his face for a moment as Ely slipped under his black cloak. "Are you still feeling the effects of the nanobots?"

Ely dismissed it with a wave forward. "I'm just getting old, my friend."

"Maybe so. How did your last physical go?" Sal asked as they entered the elevator.

"As well as can be expected for a man in his sixties."

~*~*~

A crisp November breeze greeted the pair as they stepped out onto Albany Street. A heaviness hung in the atmosphere from the cloud cover. The night air smelled like the first snow might be arriving soon.

B-dog lived just a few blocks away. He was the only Sentinel who chose not to live in the Nexus building. Instead, he lived with Julie on Pacific Street. The pair managed to cover the three blocks in no time.

Julie smiled, opening the door. "Ely, what a surprise!"

"Baby sister, it's been a while. Can we come in?"

"Of course, we're always happy to have you. Benjamin is in the living room reading." Very few still referred to him as B-dog nowadays.

Ely and Sal followed Julie further into the apartment. It had been at least two years since he'd paid them a visit. Normally, they came to the Nexus building.

"Elysian, Salvador, what do we owe for this honor?" B-dog stood, slipping his book under his arm.

Ely smiled, hoping to put him at ease. "Just a private talk, away from the ears of the Nexus."

"Please — have a seat. How can I help you?" B-dog waved his hand toward the couch.

Ely waited until he and Sal had taken seats on the sofa before he started. "We need to ask you about your last trip outside the walls. Did anything unusual happen when you were in Troika?"

"What is this about?" he asked, resuming his seated position.

Sal opted for honesty. "There were four deaths last night; all from the Black Plague."

"You're not serious. You think someone on my squad brought it back?"

"We don't know. We're trying to figure that out without pointing fingers. You know your squad better than anyone. That's why we're coming to you. Is it possible someone slipped something into your shipment without anyone seeing it? Was it ever left unguarded?" Ely quizzed.

B-dog shook his head. "Never, it went as it always does. Wait — there was a last minute box that came in for Doctor Woo. The delivery guy said it missed the original convoy, so I didn't think much about it. I just put it on the boat."

"We'll check with him next. Thank you, this could help solve the mystery to how it's been getting in." Sal stood, ready to call an end to the meeting, sending B-dog scrambling on the defensive.

"You know I'd never let it in intentionally. Doctor Woo gets herb shipments all the time. I never considered it a possibility."

Instead of letting the two old friends get heated, Ely stepped in. "None of us would. And right now, we're not accusing him or you. We're just looking into the facts. Should we find anything, we'll bring the details to the Sentinel Court for review as always. Now, we don't want take up any more your night with your wife. Thank you for meeting with us. Julie, please stop by for lunch some time. It would be great to catch up."

"I will, Ely." Julie embraced him.

He missed her. They hadn't been close in years. She had her family and he had Melanie to raise at first, then his work in the Order. Life just got in the way. With a kiss and hug, she left Sal and Ely at the door.

"Do you believe him?"

Ely ducked under his hood before stepping outside. "He looked embarrassed when he admitted about the late box."

"That doesn't make him innocent," Sal stated, clearly showing his opinion.

"Doesn't make him guilty, either," Ely countered.

"Point taken. So what now?"

"Facts. We need them. Check Doctor Woo's and B-dog's credit accounts. Are either of them depositing or spending huge amounts?"

Sal's fingers flipped the tabs around on his pad. "Nothing out of the ordinary. And there are no multiple accounts connected to their DNA."

"What about the victims? Do they have anything in common? Jobs, living quarters, friends, family, anything that would connect them in the slightest way?"

"How could victims spread over thirty years have anything in common?"

"Just do it. Let's see what the Nexus says."

It took a few seconds for the system to tabulate any commonalities. The results left them speechless and slightly paranoid. In the earlier years there had only been a handful of cases. Most of the bigger breakouts were after Melanie had left to start the correction team.

A whistle slipped from Sal's lips. "Sixty-five percent? That can't be a coincidence."

"It's not; it's murder," Ely surmised.

"Someone is murdering re-assimilated and by-product members?"

Ely huffed, stroking his chin. "It would seem so."

"Why?"

"We'll have to find the one responsible and ask them, now won't we? How far to Doctor Woo's?"

"Two blocks, that way," Sal directed toward the west perimeter.

Clapping Sal on the back, Ely nudged them toward their next destination. "Let's go have a quick chat with the good doctor."

# Melting the Snow

# Chapter Seven

## 2045

# Washing Away of Sins

"We need to get you back to the Nexus building. If the targets are connected to the corrections we've made, then you could be on their list. You fathered the team and are responsible for its inception in the first place."

"There's nothing left to take, Salvador, but if you feel safer at the Nexus, let's go."

Even as Sal led him back, Ely knew his words were true. His life had been forfeited long ago; his body just hadn't caught up yet. It couldn't fight it forever. Time wasn't on his side anymore.

The warning sirens were already sounding when Sal and Ely were ushered into the Matrix by the armed guards on duty. Something had everyone and everything freaking out.

"Straight to Nexus. Everyone needs to be shielded by the continuum capsule. The Nexus is reporting possible catastrophic time ripples pending," Jeremiah ordered as he led the way.

"What about B-Dog?"

Foster joined them from behind. "We

don't have time. We've sent a team; however, if the ripples happen before they retrieve him, we won't be able to do anything about it."

"What's causing the pending ripples?"

"Melanie. She's decided on suicide. I'm sorry, but if she does, they'll find her body, the link, and her nanobotics. Not even going to touch what it will do to her husband." Foster looked at Ely with sympathy shining in his eyes, shaking his head. "We need to override her link and send in help now. We can't wait any longer."

Ely's heart shattered. He'd done this to her. By sending her back, he'd broken her. Even though it was with the best intentions, it had backfired. Their fight in the past had added fuel to the fire.

"Override my link."

## ~2012~

Ely paced in front of the computer in the headquarters lab. His link had only stated to be there and await an urgent message from the Sentinel Order. He almost thought it was a ploy from Melanie, but then he remembered Sal saying they could override the links and that there were time tear issues with his and Melanie's recent dispute. Playing it safe seemed the better option. When he arrived, Melanie was nowhere to be found so he figured he was correct.

The computer pinged to draw his attention. He quickly dropped into the seat, cracked his knuckles, and started fumbling with the keys.

**2045: Ready for some answers?**

Ely laughed out loud. Of course, he wanted answers. Melanie had withheld them from the very beginning. Maybe now he'd finally know more about what was to come.

*2012: They're long overdue.*
**2045: The Order needs you to go to a cabin in the Berkshires.**

Frustration welled inside Ely. How would that get him answers? Was this just another ploy?

*2012: Why?*
**2045: To bring Melanie back ALIVE.**
*2012: Why wouldn't she be alive?*
**2045: She doesn't want to be.**

His frustration turned to confusion. How could she possibly not want to be alive? Life couldn't have turned sour enough for her to want to be dead. Everyone had to have something they wanted to live for, didn't they?

*2012: I don't understand.*
**2045: Trust me. Go to her. She needs you.**
*2012: Why me? Right now, I don't even like her.*
**2045: You will.**

Even Ely had to admit, he'd already begun to start forgiving Melanie after he'd spoken with Sal at the gym. Whoever was on the other end was right: he would grow to like her again one day. He couldn't guarantee the same for Melanie.

*2012: She hates me.*
**2045: Not anymore; not since you kissed her.**
**That's why the timeline shifted so drastically.**

When Ely kissed her that night, he'd never considered it might mess up anything. He could have lied and blamed the fever, but truth be told, he wanted to kiss Melanie, until everything fell apart.

*2012: Me kissing her tore the fabric of time?*
**2045: She's married.**

Ely could have kicked himself. She'd never mentioned a husband or boyfriend. No wonder she wanted nothing to do with him. In her eyes, he was a home-wrecker.

*2012: So, her husband thinks she cheated?*
**2045: No. You're her husband.**

All the air rushed from Ely's lungs. His eyes refused to blink. He waited for a new post correcting it. That had to be wrong. In the future, he was old enough to be her father! No amount of wiping his hands over his face made the words go away.

*2012: Wait — we're married?*
**2045: Yes. But there is a new threat here.**
**If the timeline is not corrected the body that replaces Melanie died here last night. That means . . .**

Ely knew what that meant. If Melanie was never sent, she'd be the one who died there.

*2012: Will my trip fix the time tears?*
**2045: We are hoping it will.**
*2012: How bad are the ripples?*
**2045: The worst we've ever seen.**
**Salvation is falling apart at the seams.**
*2012: How soon do I leave?*
**2045: NOW!**
*2012: Where do I go?*

**2045: The address will be sent to your link.**

*2012: When do we have to be back by?*

**2045: As long as she's alive, it doesn't matter.**

*2012: She's the key to fixing the ripples?*

**2045: You need to correct her and it.**

*2012: Max time you can freeze should I need it?*

**2045: 3 minutes**

*2012: Good to know.*

**2045: Ely, one thing you should know about your future.**

*2012: What's that?*

**2045: You can't have children in the future.**

*2012: Is that why I sent her back?*

**2045: Yes.**

*2012: Well, no pressure then.*

**2045: It's still your choice. Free will. You decide whether to correct that or not.**

**Her survival is not optional however.**

Ely never thought about whether he wanted a wife or kids. Now he had to consider both.

*2012: Affirmative. I'm gone.*

~*~*~

Once the screen went blank, Ely headed

out. On his way up the stairs, he shot a text to B-dog letting him know that he had been assigned a top secret mission and to make excuses for his absence at Thanksgiving Day dinner in a few days with his sister and father. His and Julie's mother had split town when his sister was only five, so it was just the three of them plus B-dog now.

Rafe got a call saying Ely had decided to start his holiday weekend sooner than planned. In his usual style, he took it fine.

It was hard not to dwell on the revealed facts from the computer conversation. For the time being, he decided to put it on the back burner since in his reality they hadn't actually fallen in love and become a couple. Though it would seem it would happen eventually. Right now, he had to accomplish keeping Melanie alive.

Ely was right; it took him two hours on his motorcycle to reach the winding roads that would lead to the cabin buried deep in the secluded woods of Massachusetts. Most of the trees were bare, but those few that still had their leaves were pretty. Doing eighty on two wheels didn't leave much for sightseeing. As Ely took the final turn, the bumps jostled the bike. The road would be rough from there in. He had to wonder how Melanie had gotten so far out there without a car. Pulling down the road, he spotted her standing by the edge of a stream. The area must be beautiful in the summer, he thought.

Melanie glanced back for a second, and then turned toward the water again. She had to be freezing in nothing but a T-shirt, jeans, and sneakers. Ely kicked down the stand and took off his helmet. Still Melanie hadn't moved. After disembarking the bike, Ely strode toward where she stood. The sounds of the raging water filled the air.

Melanie looked back once more, smiling, the late day sun reflecting the red in her hair. God, she'd never looked more beautiful. "Goodbye, Elysian."

"No, Melanie!" Ely jerked forward, yelling, but she'd already thrown herself into the churning river.

Without a second thought, he followed her into the water with his boots and leather jacket still on. Saving Melanie was all that mattered. The cold water ripped at his skin as he thrashed around and searched for her. He spotted her just ahead. Melanie didn't bother trying to stay afloat. She let the water have its way with her. It dragged her under just before he reached her. Ely drew in one last deep breath before he dove under and grabbed her by the hand as she sank to the bottom. It took a lot to tow her back to the surface, but he managed.

Holding Melanie close, Ely side-swam them both to the edge and hauled her out. She wasn't moving. Her skin had turned a pasty white and her lips were bluish.

"Melanie!" Ely yelled, checking her pulse. "Don't you leave me now!" He tilted her head back and opened her mouth. "I won't let you leave us!" In frustration, he started pumping on her chest. A sputtering cough erupted from her mouth, ejecting a mouthful of water. "You're still alive, so it's not over." Ely swept her up into his arms, cradling her to his chest. "I have to get you inside, start a fire. I need to find a way to warm you up," Ely rambled to himself, rushing toward the cabin.

Melanie's limp body lolled in his arms. Faint, misty puffs marked her slight breaths. The door to the cabin had been left ajar. Ely kicked it shut behind him. Looking around the cabin, it was easy to see it was used for rentals. He spotted her wool coat hanging over an old leather armchair in the corner of the room. He laid Melanie out on a brown bearskin rug in front of the fireplace.

A box of matches and a prefab log lay in the firebox, ready to be lit. That seemed like the best place to start. Ely chucked off his water-logged jacket and rubbed his hands together. The cold water had made them stiff. His fingers shook as he struggled to take out one of the matches and strike it against the side of the box. It took three tried to get the match lit.

Once he had the corner of the paper log burning, Ely turned his attentions back to

Melanie. She still hadn't awakened. Taking her into his arms again, he began peeling her soaked clothes away. After all her wet clothes lay in heap on the floor, his followed closely behind. He noticed that even after he wrapped his body around hers, her skin hadn't warmed yet. With his forehead resting against hers, he thought about the best ways to get her temperature up. Then it hit him: alcohol.

Ely left Melanie's side to search the kitchenette. The only thing he could find was a bottle of red cooking wine, but for what he needed it didn't matter, it would do. He grabbed a beige coffee mug from the cabinet and poured a mouthful into it. Clutching the mug, Ely rushed back to Melanie, praying it would work.

There wasn't a lot of faith left in Ely nowadays. The way his mom had abandoned them had stolen that. His father had done his best working a factory job on the third shift, but it had Ely growing up faster and helping to raise Julie when he should have been playing with his friends.

"Your nanos aren't going to like this very much," Ely whispered as his fingers rubbed the liquor on her lips. "We broke this. Together, we'll fix it."

He traced her jaw with his fingertips. Ely lowered his body back over hers and covered them both with the quilt off the faded brown couch. In that moment, he realized how close the world had come to losing her forever.

Melanie coughed but managed not to gag on the traces of alcohol. The room filled with the glowing flickers from the fire. Soon, the room felt cozy, even to Ely.

Cupping her cheeks, he asked, "Melanie, what were you thinking?"

Her eyes fluttered open and locked on his. The sheer amount of sadness locked in them was enough to knock a grown man to his knees.

"I've ruined everything," she whispered through chattering teeth.

Before she could say anything else, he crushed his lips to hers. His tongue searched for an opening. It took a moment for her to respond to his actions. Melanie slipped her shaking hands into his hair and pulled lightly before she parted her lips for him. That only excited his physical reaction to her even more.

Ely kissed his way to the sensitive skin below her ear. "Give into it, Melanie. We both need this. I can feel your body reacting to mine. Don't over think or calculate it. Just feel what my body is telling you. We can heal each other's pain."

Melanie's fingernails scratched a slow burning trail down the contours of Ely's back. "I don't want to hurt either of us anymore."

A new hunger burned in her grey eyes as

she took control, rolling them so she straddled his hips with her thighs. She interlocked their fingers and latched her lips onto his. Slight pants rattled from her chest when she pulled back and rested her forehead against his.

"Are you sure . . ."

Ely was past the point of no return. He knew what she hadn't told him. Unlocking one hand, he grabbed her hip, and merged their bodies and futures into one. With each thrust, he pushed them toward the completion that would not only guarantee pleasure in that moment, but also healing of the fissures that plagued their futures. His body was the vessel that would carry them past the uncertainty. He'd ensure they'd get Salvation and their future marriage back on track.

Melanie moved in sync with his efforts, lost in the euphoria of being connected again with the only man she'd ever loved. In that moment, it didn't matter that he'd sent her back. He'd saved her, come for her when she'd needed him, and been her savior all over again.

There would still be a lot of fixing to do when they went home. Now her heart wanted to do it. Each time he caressed her body with his movements, more of the pain and uncertainty washed away. Simple kisses spoke of promises for a better tomorrow. And when Melanie didn't think she could hold herself together a single second longer, Ely's strong arms grounded her through the ecstasy he ignited in her soul. With him, she'd found the heaven on earth she'd been searching for. Lying in his arms, fully spent, she let herself slip off to the deepest sleep she'd ever known.

~*~*~

The hours passed in silence as Ely held Melanie close. Her nanos had never activated. Ely awoke in the wee hours of the morning when his link vibrated with a message.

**Mission Update:**
**Correction waves in progress.**
**Melanie Sheppard Status Update:**
**Nanobotics and link offline**
**due to drinking the red vial.**
**She'll have to re-drink the green vial.**
**It has to be her choice.**

Ely shook his head, lifting her arm to see her link was flashing: *Inactive.*

Melanie's eyes shot open. "I had to, Ely. I couldn't risk anyone finding them."

"It didn't work. That's why they sent me. Someone did find you and them. It messed up the timeline pretty bad from what they said."

"Who said?" She pulled away, her shock clearly written on her features.

"I don't know; whoever sends the orders to headquarters."

"They sent you. Is that the only reason you made love to me?" From the bitter tone of her voice, Ely knew he'd inadvertently hurt her feelings.

He dragged her back to his embrace before explaining. "They sent me, but I'm no one's whore, Melanie. They told me to save you and that we're married in the future." Ely cupped her cheek, directing her eyes back to his. "I made my own choices after that. We'll talk this out and figure a way to get it right, together."

He'd never seen anyone look like such a scared and lost child in his life. Melanie had in spades. For some unknown reason, their lives were linked to how humanity survived in the current timeline. If they were unable to stop whatever was coming, this needed to be righted. "We'll go back, you'll re-drink the nanos . . ."

"No, I don't want to make you miserable with me anymore."

"I'm not miserable with you." Ely sighed. "Yes, I was mad before, but there is something pulling me toward you."

"It's the other timeline." Melanie tried to roll away only to be stopped in her tracks.

"What about it?"

"You're my husband there," she muttered, pulling the rug in a vain attempt to cover herself.

"I know, but I don't understand, why didn't you tell me?"

"It's not allowed. Free will and all." Melanie shook her head, a lone tear slipping down her cheek. "You know the whole 'what if you changed your mind in this timeline' thing?"

"And what if I wanted to fight for it? Which, I am apparently doing from the future!"

"What?" Melanie gasped. "That's not possible. The only reason Elysian would order for us to stay together is out of need — not love. He ordered me away to get rid of me, for Christ sakes."

"I said that? In those words?"

"No, it was implied."

"Exact words, Melanie. What did I say?"

"Your exact words were: *My journey with you ends here. This isn't the end for you. This will be the beginning of a new and long lasting devotion that will know no bounds. Follow the blackbird in flight to fulfill your destiny.* And you thought I was cryptic? Who do you think I learned it from?" Melanie lifted her eyebrow.

Ely grinned. "I got my first tattoo two weeks ago."

"What?"

"On my lower back." He rolled so she

could see.

His flesh shivered as she traced the outline. "It's a blackbird. In the future, it's covered up by the forgotten city skyline."

"I understand my hidden message. Question is, do you?" Ely rolled back and pinned Melanie below him.

She gasped with wide eyes. "So, my husband sent me back to follow you?"

"Now, I know why I felt so betrayed. The draw to you . . . I've been fighting myself and you. I'm done resisting it."

"Free will goes both ways. I can say no, too."

"You can. But we both know that is what hurt you in the first place. You thought I didn't want you. Now you know I always did."

"But I'm in love with that you. I barely know this version of you."

"I'm not in love with you either — yet. That doesn't mean it won't happen. It's proven it will, if we open up to it and let it grow."

"I don't know if I'm ready to go back yet."

Ely smiled and accepted her change of subject. "Fair enough. How about we stay here and have a long, holiday weekend? We need to work through our problems; this seems like the perfect place to do it."

Melanie mulled over it before smiling back. "I can agree to that."

"I'm going to put another log on the fire

before it dies out, then we'll grab a few more hours                              sleep."

# Melting the Snow

# Chapter Eight

## 2045

## The Rebound Effect

The walls and floors shook all over Salvation. All its residents scrambled for cover. No one knew the exact cause, but many assumed an earthquake was to blame. They weren't uncommon anymore in New England, not since the event that had started the sudden upheaval to humanity. It had been hours of everything rattling. Each timequake rolled through stronger than the last.

The Sentinels had been locked down since each arrived after the warning sirens had gone off. B-dog had been the last to join them before the capsule was sealed completely, making any entry impossible. Quinn was always the exception. His computer station below the capsule also fell under its protection.

"Ely!" Sal pointed to the red monitoring bar on the center crystalonic screen in the Nexus.

He nodded, seeing the change as well. "Whatever they've decided to do, it's working."

"You'll remember soon enough. For now,

let's just be happy that the timequakes are showing signs of slowing down," Foster said from behind his shaking station.

Sal grabbed Ely when he swayed on unsteady feet. "Time's a real bitch when she catches up to you. So, what did the younger you do?"

"More than I would have given him credit for."

Ely laughed with a grin on his face, but refused to share the new memory. Back in those days, he wouldn't have thought of sleeping with someone so quickly, but then again, the others weren't Melanie either. She definitely had something special about her.

"Quinn's reporting in." No sooner had Foster said it, the screen filled with the doctor's image.

"Nice piece of work there. Melanie's likeness has been removed from Dawnna's corpse. One problem: in the changeover, we added two more death cases."

"It would seem we have someone trying to undo our corrections. We just left Doctor Woo's lab before we were rushed in here. Someone sent him a late delivery with B-dog's team a few days ago. It cost him his life," Sal informed the room.

B-dog ignored the stares he received from the group and actively sought answers. "Did you recover any Black Plague from his lab?"

"No, if it was there, it's long gone now. We

have no idea how much came in." Ely began to pace the dark circular room. "We can't even say for sure that's what came in, but since we're sending a new body to Quinn, it's a good guess it was."

"Without proof, we can't soil his good name."

"No. Sal and I agree with you on that, Jeremiah. We keep this quiet until we know for sure."

"We've downgraded to orange," Foster updated.

A collective sigh echoed around the room.

"We need to figure out why and how someone is doing this," Jeremiah brought the conversion back to the Black Plague.

"Quinn, tell us everything you know, even if we've heard it a hundred times. Maybe something will jump out at us," Sal instructed.

With everyone's attention glued to the screen, Quinn did as asked, making sure to cover every detail until suddenly B-dog held up his hand. "Wait — the victims, besides the fact they are by-product families or re-assimilated members, why did they die if the doses are measured? Too many doses? Malfunctioning inhalers?"

"No, I'm glad you asked. The dust turned erosive when water was introduced into the victim's respiratory system."

"Like acid?" Jeremiah cocked his head.

"Exactly, turned their insides to mush, hence they bleed out."

Sal moved closer to B-dog. "What are you thinking?"

Ely could almost see the gears in the gentle giant's mind working. "The 12-12-12 underground rave Julie and I went to. We figured it would be the last time in one hundred years and we'd never see it again in our life time. At midnight, the sprinklers overhead opened up. Who knew, right?"

Sal smiled and patted B-dog on the back. "So a nightclub of some sorts? Foster, check the water consumption at midnight on the nights of the deaths; there can't be too many places using that kind of water at that hour."

"We have three possible locations. I'm marking them on the screen now."

The crystalonic screen glowed with a map of the city. Three blue circles illuminated the locations in question.

"Location one is the emergency medical center, so that's not it. Number two is the meat processing center, so scratch that one. The last spot is a restaurant named Parliament. We should send a team and have them check it out."

"And if it's wrong?"

"What do you mean, B-dog?" Jeremiah asked.

"If we hit the one place and we're wrong, the right place will be long gone before we get there. We need to clear all three of those places at the same time and on the right night. As much as you'd like to dismiss the Med Center, raves used to pop up in the strangest of places, from a moving train to an abandoned building."

"Good point. No one on the teams can know what we're looking for either. If they leak it, the plan is dead in the water," Sal agreed. "So we send in Curtis's team to Med Center under Jeremiah."

"I'll take my team into the restaurant. We need to clear our name as well," B-dog nearly demanded.

"Okay, but you hang back and watch your team. If the makers of Black Plague decide to go after Sentinels, we don't want anyone getting caught out in the open." Sal pointed to B-dog. "That leaves the meat processing center. I'll take that one with Melanie's old team."

"Nice try, Sal." Ely shook his head. "You're a vegetarian. That place will have you tossing your dinner in one glance. I'll go."

"Ely . . ."

"Who else is going to go? Quinn never leaves his lab and Foster never leaves his computer station."

"You know I hate when you're right, you know that, don't you?"

"I do. Makes up for the harassment I received when I first joined the team," Ely teased.

So much had changed from those days. Nowadays, the Sentinels weren't free to do as they pleased. Gone were the days where they wore what wanted and in were ushered the times of golden robes and governing a society that relied on them for everything.

"I think you made up for that ten times over," Sal grumbled, walking away.

## ~2012~

"Morning," Melanie whispered in Ely's ear as he stared out the window. "That can't be good."

"It's not. Mother Nature thought she'd help us out by coating the ground with three inches of snow. To most, that wouldn't be an issue, but when you're on a bike, it's a bit of a problem."

"Do you regret coming to save me?"

Everything had happened so quickly the night before that she had to wonder if in the light of day if things looked differently to him now.

"Not one bit." She melted against him when he wrapped his arms around her. "I do wish you didn't take such a drastic step with your nanobots though. What if something happens?"

Melanie could see the sincerity in his blue eyes. "One day you'll understand. For ten years, they monitored every move I've made. It was my last attempt to save them before I tried to end my suffering."

Ely wrapped the quilt around her and started leading her to the couch. "Tell me about it?"

"About my suffering?"

He pulled her down to sit with him. "Yes. What did I send you back to?"

Melanie hissed out a long breath, willing herself to be strong enough to be honest. "The traveling part hurt. That's a pain beyond explanation. Your body is literally pulled apart, molecule by molecule, and reassembled. It burns, and then you're icy cold. For two days, my insides quivered. It might not have been so bad if I had a place to go when I arrived, but I didn't. I had to hide in a subway tunnel until the effects wore off."

"I'm sorry about that." Ely wiped away a tear that slipped down her cheek.

Melanie was never fond of showing her vulnerability. She always had to show the strong side to those who followed her. Somehow, she could feel her soul healing. Things were changing. They were slight, but just enough that she could know they were on the right path. It gave her the courage to open up and let him in.

"Yeah, I know. No one considered that part." Melanie sighed. "Anyways, once I could get around, I exchanged a stone for cash and started the set up process. It took three years to get Quinn on board and the headquarters built to specs. In that time, I had zero people to talk to. No one could be trusted here. The first team member wasn't brought in until a year ago."

"So in all this time, you had no one?"

"No. At least back in my time, I had friends, a life. Here, I've only had a mission. At first, when I left, I had hoped for a second chance with you, but then over time, it just spiraled out of control. Next thing I knew, it was something I didn't recognize."

"It's okay that you hated me for sending you back, for hurting you. I can't answer for why it had to be you. The best I can manage is educated guesses, but without the facts, I just don't know."

"We should get dressed." Melanie smiled, changing the subject.

"I put our clothes up to dry. It's going to be a bit longer. I'd say I'd make you breakfast, but there's not much in the way of food here. That's going to a problem."

"Really, Elysian? You were such a skilled hunter in the other timeline." Melanie laughed, snuggling closer.

Moments like these had been few and far between in their marriage. Ely had been much older than Melanie from the beginning. He'd fought her advances in the early years, always claiming his age to be the main factor.

Finally, on her twenty-first birthday, when she'd showed up in his room naked, he allowed her to seduce him. Melanie was so lost in the memory of that first time that she wasn't paying attention to what her body had been doing until Ely moaned and gripped her hair.

"There's a bed in there." He nodded to the closed door. "This couch is too small."

Melanie giggled and jumped up. "Beat you there."

~*~*~

"Are you sure you want to run?"

"Yep, I won't have you starving. We can be there and back in a couple hours. Now hop on."

"Why are you dragging me along?"

"One — so you don't do anything foolish while I am gone. And two - I have no idea what you eat. Besides, we can have nice dinner while we're there."

"I haven't had a piggyback ride in years." Melanie laughed as she climbed on to Ely's awaiting back.

# Melting the Snow

# Chapter Nine

## 2045

## Raving Mad

Raven, Born, T.D., and Jessie needed no explanation when Ely told them to meet him at the meat processing center. They'd followed Melanie without questions for five years before she'd been sent on her mission to lead the correction team. Now, Raven headed the squad.

"Simple search, Raven, top to bottom, sub-basements included."

"As you wish." There was nothing innocent about the way she batted her heavily black-lined, spring-green eyes. "Salvador says you're to stay behind us."

Ignoring the way she flipped her long brown curls, Ely made light of the mission. "We're not expecting to find much."

"Irrelevant. Our asses are on the line here if we go back and have to report to him you have a hangnail." Raven laughed, walking away, deliberately sashaying her leather clad hips.

Everyone feared Sal with good reason. He'd proved early on, during the inception of the Order, that he'd accept no failures from the teams. His iron-fisted running kept them in line during the toughest of times.

**Mission Update:**
**Team one in place.**
**Team two in place.**
**Move in at T - :00:30**

Ely nodded to Raven from beneath his cloak for her to open the door to the meat processing center when the counter reached: 00. She strolled in like she owned the place, with the search order in her hand raised over her head.

"Good evening, folks. Sorry to bother you. It's that time of year for our standard health inspection. Please continue with your work. This will be over before you know it." As Raven addressed the employees, her team fanned out.

"The owner is off tonight," the foreman rushed up, twittering.

"This facility has passed every year. Do you think this year will be any different?"

The mousy man with geeky glasses wrung his hands together. "No, of course not."

"Good, then we don't need to bother him on his night off," Raven answered, pointing to Born to check the break room.

"That's . . ."

"Yes, it is, and it's rude to point," Raven chastised.

"Raven, we have something back here." Jessie tilted her head toward the loading bay.

Ely followed Raven to the dock to see what the discovery was. At first he didn't get it, and then he watched a young girl as she disappeared down an alley and into a manhole.

"Lock this place down before someone warns them. The rave is below us," Ely ordered, already typing a message into his link.

They needed all the teams before they could go in. Otherwise, everyone would scatter and the opportunity would be lost. Ely watched from the shadows to see others using various entry points.

"Raven, they're in the sub-basement here," J.D. reported, pinpointing the exact spot on his crystalonic pad. "Why didn't they just tell us what they were looking for? Might have made the search a little quicker."

"Don't question how the Sentinels think. There was a reason they didn't tell us. There always is," Raven snapped.

"Yes, ma'am." J.D. saluted before heading back to watch over the group of employees huddled together in the center of the room.

"You have my formal apologies. I'll be sure he's properly disciplined on his record for the disrespectful comment and tone. He knows better than to talk like that in front of you of all people . . ."

"Am I interrupting something?"

"No, Jeremiah. Where's Benjamin?"

Pointing with his finger, he directed for Ely to look out the bay doors. "With Sal. They're cutting off those exits. We're going in from here. Hopefully, we'll trap everyone in-between."

"How would you like my team to be placed?" Raven asked, standing at attention.

"For now, they're staying here with the employees. We cannot risk someone pushing a warning signal. Ely, you're to stay in the back with me."

"Sal's still coddling me, I see." Ely smiled.

"That will never change." Jeremiah laughed, checking his link. "It's time."

Curtis's team was one of the best in stealth. Watching them work only reinforced that thinking. The six person squad never made a sound as they crept down the cement stairs leading to the lower levels.

Cardboard boxes filled the spaces and lined the walls. To anyone, it looked like a standard storage room.

The team continued down to the sub-basement. Overhead and along the walls, pipes and conduits guided the way toward the boiler-room. Inching closer, they could hear the music growing louder. Everyone froze when the lead guard raised his hand. Ely typed in their readiness status and waited.

"Go!" Jeremiah ordered when the order came through.

With their rifles aimed, the squad began pushing back the stragglers into the dancing mix. The center crowd had yet to notice their intrusions.

Some of the faces Ely recognized. Under normal circumstances, they would have had their white lab coats on and looked perfectly normal. Tonight, they looked different dressed in black leather and metal studs, unshaven with their hair unwashed or spiked.

They pushed further in and corralled the groups as they gained control of the room. Ely knew they had their undivided attention when the strobe lighting and techno beats stopped suddenly.

On the center platform, Ely found the last thing he thought possible. Even with her hair blond, Ely would know her anywhere. She wore low-rise leather shorts, an up-laced leather bustier, matching black jacket, and fishnet stocking smattered with slices and cuts up the legs that peeked out of her thigh-high high-heeled boots. But it was her gray eyes that sold her out. Ely just couldn't understand how she was there.

"Melanie?" he gasped, lowering his hood.

Wearing a grin, she rolled her eyes. "Nope. Close, but no cigar, pops."

"Explain!" Sal demanded, joining them.

"Name's Mia. Melanie was my mother, which makes you —" She laughed, pointing at Ely, "— my father."

His heart raced in his chest. "How is that possible?"

"Pretty sure you know how babies are made," she teased, faking a pout.

"Where is Melanie now?" Ely had to know.

Mia squatted so she was eye level with Ely. "Dead."

"Why should we believe you?" Sal questioned.

"That tattoo of the old city skyline on his back, it used to be a blackbird. She told me when she died to find him. Free will and all. I made some new friends instead. Friends who also thought if you fucked with time it would bite you in the ass."

Ely felt like the air had suddenly been sucked from the room. Not only had she said his Melanie was dead and she was his daughter, she'd basically admitted to being involved with the Black Plague. In one moment his life had spiraled into something he didn't recognize. What had gone wrong?

"Take her. We'll figure this out at the Matrix," Sal ordered, gesturing for Ely to cover up and follow him.

~*~*~

It took over two hours to collect and transport everyone present at the rave. Every available space in the upper levels of the Sentinel High Court was occupied with interrogators as they tried to decipher who was connected and who were innocent by-standers. Mia had been found carrying four inhalers. Her guilt could be guaranteed in conjunction with her confession.

Ely and Sal had decided to interrogate her personally. They needed questions answered only she could provide.

"Breathe, Ely," Sal whispered as they waited for her to be brought in.

"We've been checking daily for Melanie to re-assimilate. I don't understand how we could have missed her."

"We'll find out soon enough." No sooner had Sal stopped speaking a knock on the door announced Mia's arrival.

Sal opened the door and nodded to the chair behind the table. "Bring her in."

If it was possible to be amused by the process, that would describe Mia's attitude. She actually smiled when the guard dropped her into the metal chair.

"I have to ask: you are enjoying this?" Sal leaned against the table.

"What's not to like? You're all scurrying around, trying to figure out if I'm lying, but you know deep in your hearts I'm not. By now, you've tested my Black Plague, and know it's real."

"It was," Ely corrected, "It's been destroyed. Where did you get it?"

"A friend made it. I'm sure you noticed many of the people at the rave work in the labs here."

"Which friend?" Sal pushed.

Mia tapped the solid metal cuffs restraining her hands off the table top. "Like the Sentinels, I don't sell out my friends."

Ely's patience for answers had evaporated. "Where is Melanie Sheppard?"

"I told you: dead." Mia rolled her eyes, actually looking bored with the whole interrogation.

"How did your mother die?" Ely slammed his hands on the table in front of her to gain her attention.

"The Arch Angels caught us in the wasteland. Like they had done to my grandparents, they slaughtered her for me to watch; of course, she stupidly screamed for you to save her as they took turns raping her first."

"No! I would have been there with her."

His anger rose in his chest. He'd never leave her behind, especially not with his child. There had to a mistake. Somehow, something went terribly wrong.

Mia leaned forward and taunted, "What did you think would happen when you abandoned her, or should I say us? Do you have any idea what those barbarians do to the children they capture? They turn them into animal bait. That's how I escaped."

"I would never do that!" Sal grabbed Ely and held him back.

"Well — you did. You were too busy saving strangers to worry about her. Ely the Heroic, to everyone except her. She really believed you loved her."

"I've always loved her," Ely declared as Sal nodded in agreement.

"We know, Ely."

"Save it, old man. I stopped believing that garbage years ago. She used to fill my head with fairy tales about how one day we'd find you. We just had to be at the right place at the right time. That time never came."

Sal released Ely and took over the questioning again, "Why are you killing people?"

Mia leaned back, smiling, apparently pleased with herself. "They don't belong here, and once I've purged the world of those like me, I'll make sure to join them in Hell."

"You'll never be able to find them all." Sal wore a cocky grin with good reason.

"Salvation," Mia laughed, "is not that big."

Ely decided to intercede, and let her in on a little known secret. "If it were just Salvation, I'd agree with you; however, we're not the only ones with teams."

She gasped, clearly shocked by the

revelation. "There are others?"

"We've set up teams in other cities as well as other countries across the globe. Melanie wasn't the only one sent back. Did you really think something this big could be achieved by five men on one correction team?"

Sirens and warning lights flashed throughout the building. Screams could be heard from various hallways.

"I think your friends are trying to break you out. That's a very foolish move."

"Would the Sentinels do no less for their leader?" She cocked her eyebrow.

"Touché. Too bad your friends don't have the same arsenal we do." Sal flipped through the tabs on his crystalonic pad. "Release the Hunters."

"The Hunters?"

For the first time, Mia showed her fear. In those moments, she looked just like Melanie. Ely's heart ached for his wife. There was no way he'd let the events unfold that way. He vowed to find a way to correct the new flawed timeline. His wife and child would be protected at all costs.

"They're cyborgs and quite ruthless. Their sole purpose is to protect the Sentinels, Matrix, and the Nexus," toyed Sal.

Ely had to know one thing before the Hunters made their way into the room and exterminated Mia. "When did Melanie and I become separated?"

Before Mia could answer, an explosion rang out, sending everyone in the room flying. Debris ricocheted off the walls and pelted everyone. The room filled with the sounds of people stepping on the fragments and their breathing through ventilator masks.

"There she is."

"Take — take him, too," Mia choked through the smoke.

Ely couldn't escape before they'd grabbed him and started towing him toward the massive hole in the wall.

"Mia, don't — this is suicide."

He neglected to mention she'd be dead even if she'd stayed. The Hunters wouldn't spare her regardless. She was now guilty by association.

"I'm dead already. I was the moment my mother died."

Ely struggled against their hold on him. "Leave me so I can save her."

"Nice try. That's the whole reason we're taking you. We don't want you messing with time and God's Law anymore," the man dragging him in the mask retorted.

Looking over his shoulder, Ely saw Sal starting to move. This would turn ugly fast once he saw them gone. The Hunters would be able to hone in on his nanobots frequencies. All the Hunters had been programmed to recognize the nanobotics of each Sentinel and to follow the commands of the Sentinels, most of all, the head Sentinel without question; unless the leader was the one under attack, then it was protect under extreme prejudice. Sal would send them on Ely's trail in minutes.

The Hunter Program was still in its experimental stage. Each soldier volunteered to be altered beyond having the nanos installed. Quinn actually brought it to the Order back in the early years, but the timing was wrong for something so bold. Technology also needed to catch up to the necessary degrees.

"This way! We're meeting up with Josie's group," the brute ordered to Mia, yanking Ely by his shoulder.

"What is she doing down there?" Mia scrambled to keep up.

"Planting a bomb in the Nexus."

"Rio, that wasn't part of the plan! You'll be killing innocents!"

"Don't get self-righteous now. We're taking out the whole hive."

Shaking her head, Mia jumped in front of Rio. "It's not just them! The blast will travel through the bridge and take out the headquarters in the past!"

"Nice friends, Mia. He's going to kill all those innocent people, all in your name and the name of God. Your mother would be so proud of you."

Mia shook her head at Ely. "I didn't know!

I would never . . ."

"Shut up, you're the one who made this mess. I'm just the one willing to make to hard choices to clean it up."

"No, you're the one willing to kill people when I'm the one who tried to save them; let's get the facts straight. If God didn't want them saved, he would have found another way to kill to them, plain and simple. There is never an excuse to murder anyone. That's God's commandment," Ely pointed out.

Rio's attention was distracted by the sounds of perfectly, in-sync marching heading their way. "What the hell is that?"

"The Hunters!" Mia screeched.

Ely froze in place. He knew better than to run. Not that it would save Rio or Mia or the others in their team. By now, they'd already be locked on the infrared tracking sensors of the Hunters mechanical visors. Red pinpoint lasers flittered across the air, searching for their targets. Servos and guns geared up as the Hunters banked the corner. Twelve soldiers clad in leather and metal armor appeared with high velocity rifles trained on the intruders.

The group scattered. One by one, they were dropped by rapid fire. Rio ran as they pelted too many to count bullets into his back. His body staggered and rocked with each impact. Mia watched in horror until he collapsed before she tried to make her getaway. With one strategic shot to her chest, the lead cyborg dropped her to the ground. Ely couldn't stay away.

With tears slipping down his cheeks, he knelt beside his daughter. "I'm sorry. I didn't know. I'll try to fix it."

Ignoring the approaching guards, Ely covered the seeping wound with his hands.

"Mom?" She reached for something to Ely's left.

"What do you see, Mia?"

"It's my mom. She's beautiful." A tiny smile curled her lips. "You were right. He does love you."

Blood dripped from the corner of Mia's mouth when she turned back to her father. "Save my mom."

Mia grasped her necklace and tugged, breaking it. She tucked it into his hands as her eyes fluttered shut to never reopen again.

"Get him to safety," Sal ordered the Hunters, coming up from behind them.

"Sir, we need to get you back."

"You need to get a team to the Nexus. They're setting a bomb."

Number one's head twitched a few times while his link flashed blue as it communicated with the other teams in the complex.

"Team three is now penetrating the Nexus. It will be secure upon our arrival."

"Ely, did she give you the details?"

"No, Sal, just this." Ely tightened his fist around the pendent of a white angel. "We'll do the best we can to send a warning." Ely wobbled to his feet.

Securely surrounded by the Hunters, Sal and Ely headed deeper into the Matrix. Stray bodies of those who had broken in littered the floors. Occasionally, one of their own would be mixed into the dead.

"Quinn's been called to the Nexus. There's been a casualty." Sal hissed out a long breath. "No report on who yet."

"Someone had to help them get in. There is no way they just walked in without a scan," Ely surmised aloud.

"I'm checking now."

"Sal . . ." Ely gasped as they entered the Nexus.

Both men froze, taking in the sight of the fallen Sentinel. It had been years since either man had seen Foster Kane out of his wheelchair. Now, the once proud guardian lay crumpled on the floor with his bloody face in B-dog's lap. The burly best friend cried over the loss openly.

B-dog always blamed himself for the accident that cost Foster the use of his legs. Of course he wasn't, and Mother Nature was, but that was a moot point. When the car they were fleeing in flipped over and pinned Foster beneath it, B-dog couldn't save his legs. Quinn did the best he could once they'd reached headquarters; however, the damage was too extensive.

"The animals beat him to death," Quinn whispered to Sal and Ely. "The Hunters have the last group pinned down in Doctor Woo's lab. It would seem they didn't get what they were looking for after all."

"Ely, look who scanned into the lab . . ." Sal held out his crystalonic pad.

"That can't be right!"

"What is it?" B-dog asked, standing to join the team.

"I searched the scans to see who helped the intruders in. It's — it's Julie."

"My wife?" B-dog howled.

"I'm sorry; she's my sister, too. Maybe they're forcing her to help them?"

"I've sent the Hunters an order to spare her for questioning. If guilty, you know the punishment as well as I do." Sal shook his head.

"Her church group."

"What about them, B?" Ely asked.

"She's been spending a lot of time with them, more than just Sunday Mass. And that late delivery for Doctor Woo, Julie was the one who accepted it." He sighed. "She asked to join me on the trip. It wasn't the first time, either."

"B, why didn't you tell me? Especially after we asked you about the trip?" Ely had to wonder if this day could get any worse.

"She's my wife. I never thought she'd bring in drugs, not once."

"Okay, we'll deal with this later. For now, let's see if she's even part of this. We're not going to hang her until we have the facts."

"Everyone, to your stations. Jeremiah, pull up the video from the lab and let's see what's going on down there," Sal instructed.

Ely pulled him to the side. There had been a nagging question that he needed answered. "Why don't I remember losing Melanie?"

"Your younger self hasn't encountered that choice yet. We can always intercede when the time comes."

"And free will?" he countered.

Sal smiled, clapping him on the back. "We'll be preventing the Black Plague."

"True."

# Melting the Snow

# Chapter Ten

## 2012

## Seize the Day

As the sun set, Melanie paced the small cabin. It had been hours since she'd awakened to a note saying Ely had taken a run to town for supplies. A chill hung in the air now that the last log was already burning low. She'd considered heading outside and grabbing a few real ones to keep it going. If he didn't return soon, that was the plan.

Headlights making their way closer drew her attention toward the road. A green camo-painted jeep turned into the driveway and parked out front. In the dark, it was hard to make out the driver until he stepped out and pulled the shopping bags with him.

Despite her best efforts to remain still, Melanie shot out the door and right into his arms. Ely laughed, dropping his bags.

"Miss me a little?"

"A tiny bit," Melanie giggled.

"I tell you what: you go heat up dinner, and I'll grab some wood from the pile over there. They were saying in town that it's going to get very cold over the next few days."

"Is that why you got the jeep?"

"Yeah, looks like I'll have to leave the bike

and come back for it when the snow clears. Hope the Order covers replacement vehicles."

Smiling, Melanie picked up the bags. "I'm sure it can be worked out."

Melanie handled the funds. They couldn't waste the money on a constant rental car; however, they could afford a purchase for one to help her to continue with the stock ups she did for the headquarters. She'd never purchased one before since she didn't have a license. Salvation was too small for cars.

"I picked up a tiny turkey and all the fixings for tomorrow."

"Oh, I forgot. You don't want to head back to be with your family?"

Melanie hadn't planned on being alive for Thanksgiving. Not that she had plans before her suicide attempt.

"Not unless you want to spend the holiday with them?"

She thought for a second before answering, "I like the tiny turkey idea if you do."

"I wouldn't have bought it if I didn't." Ely smiled at her and headed off toward the woodpile.

~*~*~

Ely's wristlink vibrated with a message just as he grabbed a log. Hissing out a sigh, he wondered if they might have to go back sooner than they thought.

**Mission Update:**
**Corrections are now in place with**
**unexpected complications.**
**Melanie Sheppard Status Update:**
**Keep Melanie within your grasp at all**
**costs.**
**If not, the white angel will be lost to**
**our side forever.**
**Her future is directly linked to the**
**killing drug Black Plague.**
**Nexus Status:**
**Unchanged.**
**Matrix Status:**
**Pending repairs from a recent assault.**
**Sentinel Status:**
**2012: 5 Active Sentinels - 2 Inactive.**
**2045: 5 Active Sentinels - 2 Deceased.**

Ely stared at the scrolling report. Why were they sending him updates? Then he remembered: Melanie's link was inactive. Surely they were meant for her, with the exception of hers. He knew that was meant for him. It didn't sit easy with Ely, and neither did the one that said deceased.

With his arms loaded with logs, Ely rushed back to Melanie. The message said not to leave her. That much he could do.

"Melanie, I'm getting weird updates on my link."

"Status updates?" she asked, coming from the kitchen with their meals.

"Yeah, I think they're for you," Ely answered absentmindedly as he dropped the wood into the log bin.

"Let's see them."

Together they sat at the small table and walked through the last three that weren't related to her. She explained the Black Plague drug, and though she tried to hide it, Ely could see her sadness over the loss of two of the Sentinels. They were her family after all.

"I hate that we can't talk back to them."

Melanie grinned. "You can."

"How? Why am I just hearing about this now?"

"Your link wasn't capable until now. While mine was active, it was the only one that could."

"So until yours is active, we can still contact them?"

"Not *we*, just you."

Grabbing her hands, Ely pleaded, "Melanie, spit it out."

"Sorry, Ely, this is one thing I can't expose. It's been forbidden for me to go into any details surrounding this level of detail in the Order. The hierarchy of the Order has to come from the way the events fall, not from me saying so."

Ely blew out a breath. "Fine, so how do

we find out what happened?"

"At the end of each message is a dot. It looks like a period." She pointed it out. "It's a hyperlink to that specific message line or status update. Tap it and a chat window box will open with a touch keypad, much like a cell phone screen."

"So which one do we want to ask about first?"

"Matrix Status, I think. See if we need to head home."

Ely nodded and did as she asked. The keys were tiny, but he managed. He had to wonder if her longer fingernails made it easier for her.

*2012: Should we head back now?*
**2045: Not necessary.**
*2012: Did we cause it?*
**2045: No.**

"Well, that was helpful."

"Try Sentinel Status, not sure they'll be willing to give more details on that one either though."

*2012: Cause?*
**2045: Rebel attack.**
*2012: Who?*
**2045: NTK**

Ely tried not to laugh at the

ridiculousness of it. Need to know? Really?

"I figured they wouldn't tell us. It would shift things if we knew. We could find a way to warn them and alter things that shouldn't be changed."

"Who decides? We change things every day." It rushed out before Ely could soften it.

Melanie tightened her hold on his hands. "Let me see if I can explain this in a better way. The changes we are already making may already change that outcome. That's one reason they aren't telling us. If we stop the event, that future will never exist, the Matrix won't be attacked, and those Sentinels will never be there to die."

"That scares me more than anything."

Melanie knelt in front of Ely and cupped his cheeks. "Why?"

"If it never happens, how do you come back?"

Ely closed his eyes. As sappy as it sounded, he meant it. He'd opened himself up to the possibility of the future with her, now he could lose her in the blink of an eye if it changed.

Melanie rested her forehead against his. "I don't know those answers. The top scientific minds in the world couldn't figure out that puzzle. Sure, they bounced around every possibility, but in the end, they couldn't say for certain what the outcome would be."

"Seize the day," Ely mumbled.

Melanie pulled back, looking confused. "What?"

"All we're guaranteed is the here and now; after that, no one knows, so we have to seize the day."

"Right. I don't know about you, but I am starving." As Melanie pulled away and stood, Ely could see her diversion for what it was: a way not to dwell on what was to come.

Nodding, he let the daunting questions running through his mind brew. "Me, too. We've got days to sort this out."

## ~2045~

The crystalonic screen in the center of the room filled with images of the inside of Doctor Woo's lab. Its inhabitants already showed the signs of feeling trapped as they paced. Both exits had been blockaded by the Hunters. Anyone stupid enough to try leaving would end up joining their fallen brethren on the hallway floors.

"She doesn't seem to be a prisoner," Sal surmised.

It didn't take long for Julie to figure out the cameras were active. Looking up with her blue eyes trained on the lens, she pleaded, "Benjamin, please, you need to let me out. Ely, I don't belong in here."

"You're not seriously going to sell us out?" whined the redhead behind her.

The shorter brunette laughed bitterly. "Of course she is."

"Shut up, Patty!" Julie snapped, leveling her a look that couldn't be seen.

"Why should I? Those monsters are waiting outside to slaughter us. Let's tell your darling husband and dearest brother how you came to us with this wonderful idea about bringing them down. I am sure they'd love to know how it was you who started the rebellion in the first place. The only reason we're even trapped in here is because you were so old and stupid that Woo had caught you using his name on deliveries."

"Not so stupid now, am I?" Julie raised her gun and popped off one shot into the stunned girl's forehead. "Fine." Turning her attention back to the camera, Julie continued, "I did it all. I'm not even sorry for any of it. If you hadn't messed with time, we wouldn't have had to go to these extremes. You left us no alternatives. God had a plan, and you went against it. What were you thinking?"

B-dog was about to answer her when Sal shook his head. "Let's hear her out."

"No doubt they were thinking they were gods," the redhead chided.

"Unless you want to be next, I'd shut up." Julie waved her gun at her friend. "Now, don't interrupt me, I'm talking to my husband. Where was I? Right! You didn't even talk to me about it; you just drank that crap they gave you. Did you even consider how I would feel about it? No, of course not. And, Ely, really? You helped recruit him. Having my brother betray God was bad enough, but to have you seduce my husband to the Devil's playground was the hardest pill to swallow. How could you do that to me? Send in your hounds, I'm not going to fight them." For the first time in Ely's life, Julie looked defeated.

Julie deliberately stepped on the pressure plate that activated the door opening. When the Hunters hesitated, she aimed her gun at them. They reacted to the threat with a sudden barrage of electric-green rifle shots.

"No!" B-dog howled, gripping his console.

Ely shook from head to toe as Julie staggered with each bullet penetration. Her comrades fared no better. Seeing the opening, the Hunters entered from both exits and began eliminating everyone left in the room. For the second time that day, Ely watched the bloodbath unfold without being able to prevent                                       it.

# Chapter Eleven

## 2012

# The White Angel

A few days in the woods did the trick. Melanie and Ely each allowed themselves to open up to the other. They spent every moment getting to know the present people they were. A few conversations strayed to the future they both knew awaited them.

Together, they prepared a miniature Thanksgiving's Day dinner. After they'd fully stuffed themselves, Ely had decided the time had come for a new adventure.

"Come with me," he said, pulling Melanie from the sofa by her hand.

"Where are we going?" She giggled, accepting the coat he passed her.

Shooting her a grin, Ely teased, "For a drive, of course. Oh, and did I mention you were driving?"

Melanie stopped dead in her tracks at the doorway. "I don't know how to drive. I told you that."

Ely tugged her out of the door way. "It's time you learned."

"Why?" Melanie croaked.

"Are you questioning my motives?" Ely opened the driver's door to the Jeep.

"You know this will end badly, right?" Melanie shot him a wicked grin.

"Only if you crack up the rental." Handing over the keys, Ely laughed.

Melanie slipped into the driver's seat. "Definite possibility."

"Just start the Jeep, smart ass."

She did as ordered and within minutes Ely had Melanie driving at five miles an hour up the long drive to the road. More than once, he said a silent prayer she wouldn't hit a tree.

"This isn't so bad!" Melanie's excitement bubbled to the surface as she gripped the steering wheel.

At first, the thought of driving scared the crap out of her. But after thinking it over for a few minutes, it made sense.

"Don't get cocky, and look out for the tree!"

"It's not me. I blame the road."

"So that's your story?" Ely raised an eye brow.

"Yep. That's my story, and I am sticking to it." Melanie laughed.

"Just keep your eyes on the road, Mrs. Earnhardt."

"Who is Mrs. Earnhardt?"

"It's a joke. You know — after the race car driver?"

"Oh, you're so funny," Melanie mocked in reply.

She knew she'd cut it close a few times to the trees lining the way, but wasn't that part of learning? It wasn't like she'd actually hit anything. By the time she reached the main road, Melanie had already started feeling more secure in her ability to drive. There were only a few times she diverted her eyes to take in the beauty of the area.

Everything looked so white and clean hidden beneath the small snow cover. Back in Salvation, snow meant hiding. The contamination would fall with the tiny white flakes. For the first year after the event, leaving the safety of the shelters brought life threatening consequences. Too many found that out the hard way.

"You're catching the hang of it." Ely grinned.

"I've watched enough to know the basics. Just don't ask me to try to park." Melanie giggled.

She still needed to adjust to the happier side of life. Over-thinking usually brought with it feelings of impending dread. Something would eventually go wrong. It always did.

With the Jeep aimed west, they headed further away from Boston.

~*~*~

By the time they were ready to head

home, a new and stronger bond had formed between the two once warring order members. On the last day, they decided to take their time driving home. Ely had suggested they visit the quaint shops in town and enjoy a nice lunch. He also planned a little surprise.

The diner's décor carried over the woodsy theme of the area. Cherry-paneled walls held picturesque artwork of the mountains, animals, and trees. Leather booths lined each wall with scattered tables in the center of the room. Tiny vases containing a single red rose balanced menus on their side.

Waiting until the waitress had taken their orders and left, Ely grinned at Melanie.

"What?" she asked.

"I bought you something to remember our time here together."

"You did? When? How?"

"Slow down." Ely laughed at her little pout. "The day I brought back groceries. It's nothing big, but I saw it in one of the small boutiques, and it made me think of you."

Ely could have sworn the pendant burned in his pocket as it awaited its new owner. He couldn't wait a second longer to see if Melanie liked it, so he reached in and pulled it out. Taking a moment to breathe, he held up the silver chain with the crystal cut angel. The charm spun, catching the light and sending multicolored fractal beams dancing across

Melanie's cheeks.

"That's so beautiful." She blushed, trailing her finger over the smooth stone.

"It won't bite you," Ely laughed.

"You really didn't have to."

"Don't be silly. Now scoot over here and let me put it on." Ely tapped the worn seat next to him in the booth.

"No one has bought me anything more than coffee in quite a while," Melanie whispered, sliding over as asked.

"Well — we'll have to work on that," Ely murmured in her ear as he draped the chain around Melanie's neck."

"Thank you," she sighed, stroking the angel pendent.

"You're very welcome."

Pride swelled in Ely's soul. Such a small gesture had made her happy. That fact was evident on her face as she smiled back at him. Too bad it didn't last. Melanie's brow furrowed as her lips curled downward.

"What are we going to tell the team?" she whispered.

"Do they know that we're together in the future?"

"Not conclusively. I'm sure Sal has an inkling." She sighed.

Ely grabbed her hand and held it. "Look, we don't have to say anything you're not comfortable with. They'll know in due time."

"You're right. I'm over-thinking this."

"One step at a time. Let's eat and head back. The rest will work itself out."

~*~*~

It had been a long day at the garage and all Ely wanted to do was head home and grab a shower. He and Melanie had plans to join B-dog and Julie to go to a midnight rave to celebrate the monumental date of 12/12/12. Melanie had come out of her shell more since they'd returned from the cabin. Ely could no longer deny his growing feelings for her, not that he tried to anymore.

Melanie had still refused to re-drink the nano cocktail. Her claims of needing more privacy time seemed to Ely like an excuse. For whatever reason, she didn't want to deal with those in the future sending the updates.

Ely hissed when his link vibrated against his wrist. Was it too much to ask for a little peace?

### Mission for Ely and Melanie:
### Retrieve your bike from the cabin by midnight.

Tapping on the hyper-link, he couldn't imagine why the rush.

*2012: Can't it wait?*
**2045: No, by midnight.**

*2012: We had plans.*
**2045: Had being the operative word.**
*2012: Affirmative.*

Before he could call Melanie, she called him first. She'd received the same message on the mission computer at headquarters. Though she didn't like doing it, she still had to communicate any incoming missions to the teams from the main source to their links while Ely worked. They decided to leave after rush hour traffic and eating. He even squeezed in a quick shower before driving over to pick her up at nine-thirty p.m.

Ely had smiled when Melanie hopped into the jeep. He didn't miss the nervousness. Even though she smiled back, it was forced.

The two hour ride passed in a tensed quiet as Melanie fidgeted in her seat. Ely had asked her about her anxiousness, but she merely blamed it on the day. He knew she was hiding something; he also knew pushing her would only get her to recoil.

Turning down the road, Ely reported, "We're here."

"There's the bike." Melanie pointed to the where it was still chained and locked to the metal frame of wood bin.

"Get into the driver's seat. You're going to follow me to the rental place. They're closed, but I called and told them we'd leave the jeep in their lot with the keys locked inside," Ely explained, getting out.

"I still don't have a license," Melanie fretted as she joined outside the car.

Ely laughed, slapping her ass in passing. "Then don't get pulled over. Just remember what I taught you and you'll do fine."

"One lesson isn't going to fool anyone."

"Another reason I chose for us to do this so late: less cars on the road and chances that we'll come across any police," Ely rambled, unlocking the padlock and unraveling the chain.

"Wish me luck." Melanie gripped her angel charm and smiled as she slipped behind the wheel.

"Luck," Ely laughed, mounting the bike.

With a turn of the key, Ely had the rebuilt 2007 black-cherry FJR1300A Yamaha purring to life. It took a year of weekends to put the motorcycle back together after the previous owner had wrecked it and tried to repair it on his own.

# Chapter Twelve

## 2045

## Twelve

"It's time. Salvation is on the verge of shaking itself apart," Sal called the Nexus control room to order. "Our five other eastern continent communities are reporting the same tremors. It's safe to say it's global."

Quinn nodded from behind his station. "Let's hope we did enough."

Ely looked to the two empty consoles. "Melanie and Foster will hopefully be with us in the adjusted timeline."

"We should have told her the truth about the others and their teams. Maybe she wouldn't have felt so alone there."

"Jeremiah, we couldn't risk it. If she sought out Ian in San Diego or Jon in Montreal, it could have caused even more unexpected equations to develop," Quinn retorted without looking up from his calculating on his screen. "It's one reason we each had a team that reported directly to one of us. There would be no cross contamination of information between them."

B-dog grimaced. "Who's going to notify Foster's team?"

"As planned, his control reverted back to the master link upon his death."

"How did you decide who'd receive the master wristlink anyways?" Sal quizzed.

"I didn't, and I never told Melanie, it was a crapshoot." Quinn laughed.

"Great, now you tell us," Jeremiah chided.

Ely had to ask, "Would it have mattered back then?"

"I doubt it."

"Quinn, it's also time to get the other six Sentinels on the center screen," Sal ordered.

Our European counterparts were connections of Quinn's department at MIT who were teaching abroad. Lynx Lambert had been the one to be sent back to recruit them and set them up, as Melanie had done for the team in what would be Salvation.

Celestial was set inland of what once was France in Le Mans.

The images of Victor, Shamus, Rosie, Brian, Rebekah, and Lynx filled the room. It was plain to see their control room shook as well.

"It's time to warn your teams to head for their headquarters. Each headquarters was specifically set up in a known safe zone."

"Are you sure nothing more can be done, Ely?"

"We're sure, Victor. Our teams will be getting the same orders shortly. Every effort has been made for a better tomorrow."

"Everyone saved has received enough hints funneled through outer channels to help them along the way. Let's pray it was enough," Quinn added.

"The first event triggers at twelve a.m. eastern standard time. Once it begins, the cascading effects will spiral outward. Some of our memories will be altered from that point depending on our interactions with those we saved. I just want to say it's been an honor and a privilege to have known you all in this timeline." Ely spoke from the heart.

"The honor was ours," all six said in sync as they bowed their heads.

## ~2012~

Melanie waited for Ely to strap on his helmet and to pull out first before she followed him, heading toward the rental dealer. Her nerves had been on edge all day, ever since she'd had the extensive conversation with 2045 regarding what would be heading their way. There had never been a time when keeping secrets had been so hard. Since she and Ely had taken the next step, it felt like lying when she withheld knowledge from him.

So much preparation and hope had gone into preparing and praying tomorrow would never happen. When word came in today that they'd failed, Melanie's emotions were all over the place. She never wanted humanity to live through what was headed their way. Now, nothing would change it. The countdown to the event had begun.

At least she'd said her piece to those in the future as it was now. Once the event happened, the new choices would change 2045 and those she knew. They all needed closure before their time was over. Salvation had been steadily moving into the red as pending timequakes began building that morning. As she drove, Melanie remembered each Sentinel's final message.

**2045: Bring them home to the fold.**
**Hugs. *B-dog***
**2045: We know you did your best.**
***Jeremiah***
**2045: See you soon. *Sal***
**2045: Don't redrink your nanobots**
**until my younger self gives the go ahead.**
***Quinn***
**2045: Stay by my side at all costs. *Ely***

~*~*~

Melanie's hands trembled as she pulled the jeep into the spot next to where Ely sat on his bike, waiting in the lot. It was already ten-thirty and time to get home would be tight. Since they planned to take the bike home under orders, Melanie hopped out and rushed over to follow her personal orders from her husband. He had to know something she didn't. Over the years, she'd learned he always had a reason.

"Ready?"

"Yeah, as ready as I am ever going to be."

Melanie tried to return his smile when he passed her the spare helmet to wear. She'd never ridden on a motorcycle after what had happened with the Arch Angels and her parents. Just the sound of Ely revving the motor brought forward accelerated breathing and panic. Swallowing a sharp breath, Melanie tried to bury the memories to the back of her thoughts. Tonight would be hard enough without them.

"What aren't you telling me?" Ely asked when she slipped on behind him.

"I don't know what you mean?" Melanie lied.

"I know something is up. You're acting all nervous. Is it something I need to know?"

Closing her eyes and burying her face into his black leather jacket, she knew she couldn't keep it from him any longer.

A lone tear slid down her cheek. "We failed. The Order has cut us loose until after the event. We're on our own for however long it takes to reconnect."

"When? When does it happen?" There was no mistaking the fear in Ely's raised voice,

"12/12/12 at 12:12 A.M. That's why the

event is referred to as Twelve."

"What's going to happen?"

"Ely . . ."

"If we didn't fix it, why can't I know?"

"Choices. You'll make different choices if you are warned."

"Where do we need to be to be safe?"

"Headquarters. All the team members and anyone saved were sent an email remotely thirty minutes ago. It was the best we could do. Now the choice is theirs to heed the warning or not."

"Hold on tight." Ely yelled, popping the clutch and screeching the tires.

Melanie had barely enough time to lock her fingers together before the bike skidded to the left on their hasty departure.

The empty night air filled with the sounds of the motor throttled to the maximum. Several times, Melanie gasped in fear when Ely would jerk the motorcycle to either side to avoid any obstacles in their path. Every taut muscle in his back could be felt through the leather jacket he sported.

They'd just reached the top of one of the largest hills on Route 2 when both their alerts sounded off. Ely brought the bike to a fishtailing stop in the break down lane. Time had run out.

The ground began to shake beneath Melanie's foot as she stepped off. Ely joined her just in time to see the few cars on the road swaying as they also tried to stop. Several vehicles careened into each other. Drivers and passengers alike staggered from their cars to try and see what the disturbance was. Wrapping his arms around her, they stood clinging to each other and took in the sights and sounds of the Twelve event.

The deafening roar of shifting earth set off every alarm for miles. Melanie's attention snapped skyward. A gray mushroom cloud rose into the night sky far to the north.

"An earthquake!" Ely yelled over the rumbling.

From their vantage point, the couple could see the silhouetted buildings along the route trembling. The tallest among them violently swayed until they slipped out of sight. Boston's barely visible sky line faded into a giant plume of dust.

"No!" Melanie's finger shook as she directed Ely to look northward again.

Ely's jaw went slack at the sight of the blazing red and orange burst where the cloud once rose from. Glowing tendrils danced high, reaching at least a mile into the sky. The pair staggered when a rolling wind ripple threatened to knock them off their feet. Ducking down on his haunches, Ely brought them closer to the safety of the humming ground.

"A volcano!" he hissed into Melanie's hair.

She sighed as the jarring shifts slowed.

"Mount Ossipee."

Ely raised them both back to standing. "That's why the world crumbled? How does one exploding volcano in the northeast devastate the world?"

"It doesn't. Right now, the tectonic plates across the globe are shifting in response to this one. New Hampshire is now a wasteland. Only hundreds survived. Boston, Rhode Island, and Connecticut are in ruins. New York," Melanie checked her watch, "has just begun its implosion from the 10.3 quake that is hitting it. There is no help coming because in five minutes there will no Washington, D.C. to save us. By morning, the entire Northern Continent and all of Mexico will fall."

Ely gripped his hair and tugged at it. "What about Europe?"

"They fair slightly better than we do. A wall of water is already headed their way. Their Twelve event strikes at 12:12 p.m. their time."

"So there never was a hope of stopping it," Ely grumbled, kicking at the gravel beneath his feet.

Melanie gripped his arm in an effort to regain his attention. "Everyone saved who listened to our warning were slipped information anonymously in an effort to open their eyes. It would appear it didn't work."

"We need to get back to MIT. Help those

we can."

At midnight, Dr. Quinn had already moved all his research to the headquarters computers. Per his emailed instructions, the nanos had been drunk an hour prior. Knowing everyone would be rushing to the sanctuary, he'd decided to wait above for them to arrive. Still shy of all the facts, he had no idea what to expect. What he saw boggled his genius mind.

Quinn fell back against the building's outer wall when the slight shaking began. New England had had minor earthquakes before. He expected it to settle quickly. What he didn't expect was for it to continue to increase in strength. A deafening roar filled the air. His focus darted to the buildings across the river. The skyscrapers soon began to sway. Shattering windows and screams from anyone out on the crisp December night joined the sounds of chaos. Before he could react, two cars flew into the parking lot and slammed on the brakes in front of him.

B-dog and Julie exited the first car at the same time. While Julie ran toward the door, B-dog and Sal started dragging an unresponsive Foster from the back of the second car.

"What the hell happened?"

"We were rushing here when another car flipped our car. Sal and Jeremiah were both right behind us. Once we pulled him from under the car, we raced here as fast as we could. Doc, his legs?"

Quinn knew right away that, even with the nanobotics, there was no saving the mangled mass of limbs. The damage was far too devastating.

"Let's get him downstairs. My lab is up and ready to go. However, I really don't know how much I can save." Honesty seemed like the best policy given the extent of carnage remaining.

Sal, Jeremiah, and B-dog nodded, scooping up their fallen team member. Each wore their fear on their faces. But before anyone could take a step, a heated, debris filled, rolling blast of air bowled them off their feet.

Wiping the soot from his face and looking up, Quinn gawked at the once picturesque skyline. It was gone. Nothing remained but massive mounds of flaming rubble. The usually calm waters separating the space churned and boiled. Quinn knew this was no simple earthquake. This was the defining moment to all of mankind. Whatever they did now would decide if there would be a future for humanity at all.

"Doc?" Jeremiah's hand stretched out for him to take.

"Thank you," he mumbled, accepting the help back to his feet.

That was the hidden answer to everyone's fate. Stand together, or fall alone.

**~The End of the Beginning~**

# Melting the Snow

# *Epilogue*

## ~2045~

Ely stretched out in his bed, wincing at the residual pains that never ceased. He smiled when the bed shifted from someone else's presence.

"Why hasn't the pain from the bots stopped? You shouldn't be suffering this long," Melanie asked as she reached out to hold him.

Thinking back to the days after Twelve had killed off two-thirds the population, Ely knew the time had come. Honesty was the best policy. "I'm dying. I knew it before you left."

Melanie bolted up in bed, gasping. "Then why did you send me back? Why waste the last few years we had?"

Ely chuckled and pulled her back into his embrace. "To give us more time. I knew we couldn't correct the 10.3 quake. There was no one single event to stop. Don't you understand? The earthquake was only the first of many events that led to our future downfall. But, by sending you back before you were too old, it gave us a whole other life together and a child before the radiation from the Technetium that took my ability to have children; and when we met you as a child, it gave you a mother. So you see it was always about giving you what I couldn't in this life. I never stopped loving you, Melanie."

"I've always loved you, too, Ely. Thank you for both Melanie and Hope. You and my children    are    my    life    now.

# Author Biography

Michele Richard is an author and the CEO of Renaissance Romance. Michele wrote the "Mocked by" series including *Mocked by Destiny* and the *Mocked by Faith* trilogy. She writes what comes from the heart. Raised in Maryland, Michele currently resides in the Boston area.

When Michele is between books, her days are filled with family and friends. Her greatest passions are traveling and learning new languages. She is currently learning French, Spanish, and ASL, and one day hopes to be fluent in them. She has never met a language she didn't like.

In 2012, Michele opened Renaissance Romance Publishing.

**Her Works Include:**

*Mocked by Destiny*
*Mocked by Faith*
*Mocked by Faith ~ Healing the Faith*
*Mocked by Faith ~ Affirming the Faith*
*Parasouls: Divine Intervention*
Changes of the Heart (*Life is More Than Candy Hearts*)
10 Days to Love (*Harvest Treats*)
The Roommates (*Sugarplum Dreams*)